THE
SHARK
DID
IT

SOUTHERN
BEACH
MYSTERIES

THE
SHARK
DID
IT

KAY DEW SHOSTAK

Kay Dew Shostak

THE SHARK DID IT

ISBN: 978-1-7350991-4-9
SOUTHERN FICTION: Cozy Mystery / Southern Mystery / Florida Mystery / Island Mystery / Empty Nest Mystery / Clean Mystery / Small Town Mystery

Typeset and Cover Design by Roseanna White Designs
Cover Images from www.Shutterstock.com
Editing by Jessica Hatch of Hatch Editorial Services
Author photo by Susan Eason with
www.EasonGallery.com

Published by August South Publishing. You may contact the publisher at:
AugustSouthPublisher@gmail.com

Dedicated to my mama, Evelyn Chancey Dew,
and her new adventure living on our island.
If I turned her into a character in one of my
books, no one would believe she was real.
You are never with her that you don't laugh.
The hardships she's encountered are just part
of her story and nothing she dwells on.
My daddy and she created the marriage God
had in mind when he came up with the idea.
She's a storyteller, curious about everything,
and the best woman I've ever known.

And as always,
To our home –
Amelia Island and Fernandina Beach
While Sophia Island and Sophia Beach
are based on you,
the characters and situations
can only be found in my imagination.
Oh, and in my books.

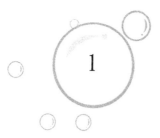

1

"The last thing I want is a birthday party." Eden huffs as she lugs a full basket of folded clothes out of the laundry room. She drops it with a loud thud at the bottom of the stairs and then comes into the living room where I am. "Twenty-five was fun, and I was still young. Twenty-six sounds old and almost thirty." She falls into the chair across from me.

My young roommate, because twenty-six is most definitely young, is in a funk. At least that's what we old people call it. Her dark red hair is longer than it's been since she moved in with me six months ago, and her roots are a tamer red, like her mother's. Eden tans surprisingly well for a redhead, and so her floral tattoos, including the pink flower on her cheek, don't stand out, which I actually kind of miss. It was cute how the color of its petals would intensify with her blush when she was mad or happy. Now it's a blah, muddy mauve to match her mood.

"You're not old, and you don't have to have a birthday party. That's why I told you that your dad stopped by with his idea." I gather up the paint sample cards on the coffee table in front of me and stack them together.

She suddenly sits forward, her elbows planted on her knees and her head in her hands. "Dad," she growls. "Dad is just trying to make Mom feel better. She's been in a funk since May and all that junk with Victor Morrison. She went from knowing everything about everything to knowing nothing."

Young people still use the word "funk." Noted. "Yeah, that's what he said. But honestly, Victor fooled everyone. Look at us: he was here putting in the air conditioning the whole time, and we didn't figure it out." I can't suppress my shudder. "Heck, Lucy got close enough he almost killed her."

"But Mom prides herself on being so sensitive and being able to read people." Eden looks up at me, and there's a bit of her old energy and spark back. "She thinks she was a fortune teller in a previous life."

With a chuckle I admit, "I could see that with Kerry. Listen, it's only been a couple months since all that happened. She just needs more time."

"And a party. Dad's right: She needs a reason to bake. She hasn't turned on the oven all summer, she keeps telling me. Telling everyone. She's proud of it, like she's doing some kind of penance." Eden stands up. "Speaking of penance, I have more clothes to fold. Can't believe I let it all pile up like that. I had to wear one of my old high school track shirts to work yesterday. It was okay because it looked retro"—she wrinkles her nose—"but it smelled like it too." She drags herself to the basket of clothes, then sighs as she lifts it and again while clomping up the stairs.

"She makes me tired," I mumble. When Eden moved in, it was to help me clear out the furniture that was crammed into this old house. She also provided me with some energy, but these days she's more of an energy drain. As I look around the room, it's hard to remember what it looked like in January when we moved in. Craig's long-forgotten aunt left him the Mantelle Mansion, which had been closed up for at least ten years after she checked herself into a nursing home. Before that she'd lived here alone, except for those summers Craig, or C. J., as the locals called him, spent on Sophia Island as a boy.

Laying alongside the stack of paint cards, my phone jingles and a picture comes up on the display. "There's my baby," I say, picking it up and thumbing through the morning pictures my daughter Erin sends each day of her new baby, Ellie. Ellie came just a bit early, so she arrived the same day I arrived in St. Louis for a visit: August 10. My flight to St. Louis was supposed to let me get there a few days before she did, so I missed being at her birth, but that's all I missed. I stayed for a week and got back a couple of days ago. Erin, Paul, and Ellie are doing great, and I miss them, but I have to admit I missed my island too. This summer has been full and yet so calm and peaceful. Oh, and hot. So hot, but the new air conditioning makes all the difference.

Both of my sons came and stayed with me for a few weeks over their summer break. Chris is even looking at doing his graduate work in the area. Of course they also went to see their dad, who is still working in South Florida. Other than the boys' travels and Ellie's arrival, Craig and I haven't really talked.

It's just hard doing all that relationship stuff long distance. And hard to find reasons to put ourselves through it.

There's a knock on the door, and at the same time Eden barrels out of her room above me. Then she's barreling down the stairs, yelling, "Don't answer that! I'll get it." She flies by me raving, "It's Aiden, and he's lost his mind!"

I stand. This feels like something I want to be standing for. Besides, I seriously doubt Aiden has lost his mind. He's my best friend's son, a police officer, and Eden's longtime boyfriend. Never in the eight months I've known him has he seemed like the type to lose his marbles.

She wrenches open the heavy front door, and sure enough there's the crazy man in his police uniform, literal hat in hand, sporting puppy-dog eyes. "It's my job," he begins. "I had to, Eden. It was just a couple of questions."

Eden bursts into tears. "You know my mom isn't feeling good. Why can't you just leave them alone?" She runs back past me, pushing me away when I try to stop her, and then she dashes back up the stairs, ending her tirade with a slammed door.

"What in the world is going on?" I ask

Aiden as he closes the front door behind him and stands there looking more angry than sad, now that the reason for the puppy-dog eyes has fled back upstairs.

"She doesn't get my job. She thinks I can pick and choose what I do. Matter of fact, I did pick and choose this. I thought it'd be better coming from me than from some stranger. Ted Church is not the most stable person on the face of the earth, and Kerry is more than a little weird, I think you'd have to agree."

I choose not to take the bait. "What would be better coming from you?" I move closer to him so we can talk more quietly.

"She didn't tell you? Any of it?" He sets his jaw and takes a minute to breathe through his nose. "There's an investigation. Apparently some kid got a tattoo from her folks a while back. There were complications and he died."

"From a tattoo?"

"I don't think so, but do you think Eden cares what I think? No, she wants me to refuse to do my job. Probably we'll look into it and it'll all go away, but she wants it to just *magically* go away. She's unreasonable, and I've had it." He whips around, jerks open the door, and heads across the porch.

I follow him into the afternoon heat. "I'll talk to her. She's just having a rough time right now."

At the bottom of the steps, he half turns back toward me and shrugs. "Whatever. Like I said, I've had enough." I watch him walk to his car, and then I go back inside and look up at Eden's door. Funk explained.

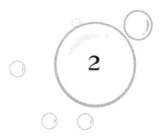

2

"I guess with me being in St. Louis I missed that they were having problems. I knew he hadn't been over since I'd been home, but..." I shrug and dip my grilled shrimp in remoulade sauce.

Annie shakes her head as she takes a bite off her hushpuppy. We're having dinner on the porch at the Dunes Restaurant—and dying. Even with the ocean breeze, the heat is intense, and we aren't wet like all those around us wearing bathing suits.

Correction: *I'm* dying; Annie is fine. She has on a loose, sleeveless cotton shift dress, as do I, but she's not sweating a bit. I'm dripping into my remoulade. She convinced me once we sat down I'd be fine. I'm not. I'm dying.

She heaves a sigh. "Yeah, those two have not had a good summer. Annabelle got that internship with the TV station in Jacksonville and moved down there with a friend, so that left just me and Aiden in the house." She raises her eyebrows at me. "That hasn't gone too well for me or Aiden. Didn't realize what a buffer Annabelle had been. And then there's all that stuff with Eden and her folks."

"But what about this kid dying from a tattoo?"

Annie's head jerks up. "What kid?"

Oops. Guess that's not common knowledge. "Oh, just something Aiden said. But Aiden said he didn't think it was the tattoo, so never mind."

"A kid died?"

"A while ago, he said." I look around for our waiter and try to derail this train. "I need some more water. You want anything?"

"Yeah. Details. How could a tattoo kill anyone?" Annie doesn't sweat the heat, but when it comes to island news, you could call it gossip, she doesn't play around. She pushes her plate away, and her collection of silver bracelets jangles as she plants her elbows on the table, laces her fingers, and stares at me.

"I just said Aiden doesn't think it did. There's our waiter. Can I get some more water? Ice too." Our waiter nods at me and immediately heads back inside. I fan myself with my napkin. "I'm burning up. Why are we eating out here?"

"Duh, the ocean is right there. Look at all these people. They paid to get to come here for a week and eat shrimp on the sand. Not that we're sitting down there on the sand. That's just crazy."

The restaurant has a wide covered porch right in line with the dunes, so diners have an unobstructed view of the beach. Between the porch and the ocean are a couple of rows of picnic tables with umbrellas actually sitting on the sand. It's a very popular place for sunbathers to eat as it's just a short stroll from their beach chairs and towels.

"Can I get you ladies anything else?" our waiter asks after filling my water glass.

We tell him, "No," and he lays our check face down on the table. I settle back in my chair to try and relax. I think that's my problem: I don't know how to just sit still and relax. I take a deep breath and look out at the waves and try to steer away from the tattoo thing. "I think Eden and Aiden will be okay. It's just a rough patch."

Annie sniffs. "Honestly, I think your

boys being here this summer is part of Eden's problem."

"Chris and Drew? Why? What did they do?"

Annie pats my arm. "They didn't do anything per se; they're just so *collegiate*. They didn't have to report for duty early in the morning, so they could stay out late and just be, well, fun."

"Eden didn't even hang out with them that much." Although, now that I think about it, she was out of the house more than normal, and if they weren't there, she wasn't either. I sit up straighter as Annie studies our bill. I keep defending my boys. "They're younger than she and Aiden are; they should be more carefree. And they were on vacation."

"Of course." She busies herself getting into her wallet, but her mouth is firmly closed and she's avoiding looking at me.

I take out a twenty and put it on the tray. "He can just split it evenly and keep my change." I chance a look up and see that she's still pouting. "Seriously. What's going on?"

She rolls her eyes; they are large and dramatic, just like their owner. "It's an age-old story: The summer kids are all fun and games. The town kids have jobs and responsibilities." She throws up her hands and lets them drop to her sides. "Ignore me. I'm in a mood too. I hate when the kids go back to school. Markie and Leah won't be coming over and spending the night since they live all the way over in Callahan, and I got used to being with Adam's kids a lot during the week."

"It's crazy to me that the schools down here start back so early."

"Oh, I know! For crying out loud, it's still summer, but nobody cares what I think." She shoves her chair back. "You ready? They've got a line of people waiting for tables."

We make our way through the crowd of vacationers and out to the sidewalk along the parking lot and beach, where a row of benches is placed. The sun sets on the marina side of the island, but the reflection of the pink-and-orange sky over the ocean is soft and inviting. I nod toward the waves. "Want to sit for a minute?" I lead us down the sidewalk to the benches at the end. "It's quieter down here."

There's a beachside park behind us and another big restaurant behind that, but we're far from any dining chatter that's not already lost to the wind, waves, and seagull screeches.

We sit and Annie chuckles. "I thought you were burning up."

"Oh. I was. Guess it's breezier out here."

"And you forgot about being hot when we got to talking about your boys. That's the trick: ignore the heat." She shoots her finger at me and winks. "Naw, your boys are delightful. If anything, your boys showed both Aiden and Eden they need to make some decisions. They aren't kids anymore." She sighs and shakes her head. "But you know how some kids just don't want to grow up? That's my Aiden."

"Oh, I don't know about that. He's a police officer after all."

"Living with his momma. Anyway, so about this kid that died. Why don't I know about that?"

"I don't know."

For being a larger lady, Annie makes jumping up from a park bench look remarkably easy. "Let's drive by Charlie's on the way home and ask him. Besides, he was putting in that porch swing, and we need to see it." She starts toward the parking lot, saying loudly, "I know! We can stop and get ice cream to take over there."

I don't jump up, but I do unfold and follow her. I don't think I'll mention that I've already seen, and tested, Charlie's new swing.

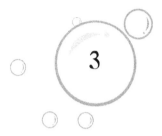

3

"When are you going to do something about this kitchen?" Annie asks. She's standing at Charlie's counter sticking spoons in the three Styrofoam containers of ice cream we stopped and got at Tribiani's drive-through. I'd been in the bathroom, and I slide into a seat at the small kitchen table.

Hands on his hips, Charlie looks around. "Why? What's wrong with it?"

She hands us our bowls and turns back to get hers. "You don't think it's a tad too pink for a guy?"

Charlie bought his house at the beginning of the summer when he separated from his wife. He bought it from Timothy Raines after Raines's mother, Amanda, died in the spring. It's just outside the historic district and in a jumble of older houses; some small, some sprawling, some updated, many not, across from the railroad yard for one of the paper mills. There are even a number of newly built homes, but this isn't one of them. Inside, the house looks like a woman lived here alone for several years. Which she did. There is a preponderance of pink paint and floral wallpaper. Most of the furnishings came with the house, and they carry on the fluffy, lacey, girly vibe. Besides all that, it's a nice house on a very sheltered lot with big trees, bushes, and basically jungle surrounding it.

He points at the pink backsplash. "Kind of figure unless I take out all that tile I'm stuck with pink. As long as everything works, it's good with me. I may not agree with Amanda's decorating taste, but everything she left is quality."

Annie studies the room as she walks to the table. "It does all look pretty new. Yard's kind of dense, but Amanda didn't strike me as an outside kind of lady." As she starts to sit down at kitchen table across from me, she asks, "Or do we want to go out to the screened porch?"

Charlie shakes his head. "No way. You're right that Amanda didn't spend much time outside, and the screen has holes in it that the mosquitos know all about. Here's good." He pulls out a chair, sits, and we eat our ice cream in silence, though I can feel Annie studying me and our host.

She finally asks, "So, Jewel, what do you think of the swing?"

I shrug, but my shrug is stopped with my shoulders lifted when I look up and see her eyes twinkling. She adds, "Do you think the sunset view will be good from it?"

I shift my eyes to Charlie. He nods. "She knows you were here last night to see the sunset."

Annie laughs again and beams at me. "You didn't tell me you were in the habit of stopping by to visit Officer Greyson."

"I was taking a walk, ran into Charlie, and we came by here so he could show me the swing." His home sits facing the railroad, which gives a good view of the sunset if you don't mind looking around a huge mountain of woodchips or having the paper mill in the background. He'd only put in the porch swing yesterday, so it made perfect sense to wait and see what the sunset looked like last night when we ran into each other. I explain all this to Annie, but I'm not sure she can hear me when she's grinning so big.

"Sure. Sure! It's mighty convenient y'all being neighbors like this."

Charlie finishes his last bite and sets his empty cup down. "I like living where I can take a walk. I always wanted to live in a neighborhood." I glance up just in time to see him wink at me. I'm glad Annie missed it, as she's getting the last of her ice cream onto her spoon. I have a feeling as soon as she's no longer distracted by ice cream, she's going to really amp up the matchmaking.

I scoot back and say, "Well, I guess we should be going."

But Annie interrupts. "We want to know about this boy that died from one of Ted's tattoos. What happened, and why haven't we heard about it before? Where's he from? Do we know his people?"

Oh, I'd forgotten about that.

Charlie holds up a hand. "Whoa there. Nobody said he died from a tattoo. That's why we're doing an investigation. No, you don't know him or his family."

"You sure about that? I know a lot of people." Annie tries again. "Where's he from?"

Charlie gets up, collecting our bowls. "Annie, leave it alone. Did Jewel show you the pictures of her new granddaughter?"

"Of course she did. Ellie's a doll." She

pushes up from the table, no jumping this time. "You know we've been awful helpful in some of your recent investigations. We might could help with this one too."

Charlie sighs and turns to throw the bowls into the garbage. Then he stops, leans on the corner of the cabinet, and looks straight into Annie's face. "It's more to ease a family's grief than it is an actual investigation. It's sensitive enough without Ted flying off the handle and you sticking your nose in, understand?"

She huffs and rears back, then demands, "Jewel, you ready?" She jerks her head to look at me. "Or did you fall asleep over there? You're being awful quiet about everything tonight, aren't you?"

"Sorry. I'm ready to go." I hurry to the side door.

Annie sniffs as she passes Charlie to show her annoyance with him one more time. We step out into the evening, which is noisy with bugs and frogs. The corner lot is lit up from the streetlamps, but outside that cone of light, there are a lot of dark shadows. I forge on ahead to Annie's car in the gravel driveway.

Charlie follows us and gruffly says, "Sorry, Annie, but Aiden should not have mentioned it to you."

Great, now I have to fess up. I stop and turn to face them both. "It was me. Eden's parents told her, and she got mad at Aiden. They had a fight, which I overheard. I didn't know it wasn't common knowledge, so I mentioned it to Annie."

Charlie's stern look changes to something more forgiving, with a lift of his eyebrows and the beginning of a smile. He nods. "Oh, that makes sense. You didn't know."

Annie looks from me to him, then throws her hands in the air. "For crying out loud! It's all okay now?" She shakes her headful of shiny, silver curls and marches to the driver's side door. "Let's go. We can't dillydally out here; the bugs will eat us alive."

We climb into her car, and the doors are barely closed before she claps her hands and laughs. "Law, child, that man has it bad for you. How's his divorce going? Charlie and Jewel sitting in a tree." She bursts out laughing. "No! Charlie and Jewel sitting in a *swing*!" She laughs all the way to my drive-way.

I should've walked and dealt with the bugs.

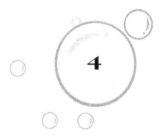

4

"She looks familiar," I mumble to Tamela as we arrive at our table for our weekly group lunch. We're just off the island at Bridge's, which I thought got its name because it's underneath the big bridges crossing over the river onto the island. Now that I'm here for the first time, I see there is also the railroad bridge that runs right alongside the restaurant's decking. We got here just as a train was crossing, and then we got to see the bridge open back up for boat traffic.

I rode with Tamela and Charlotte, and as we arrived, Charlotte peeled off to talk to two ladies at another table.

I guess Tamela didn't hear me. As I take my seat, I nod toward the small table and speak up. "The lady Charlotte is talking to looks familiar."

Tamela rolls her eyes at me, sits down, and then leans in close to whisper, "She should. That's Galena Bellington, and you spied on her in her house through holes in the wall."

"Oh yeah." I sit up straight and pick up my menu, holding it high to block my face. When Craig and I first moved here, Charlotte Bellington, an older member of our group who depends on Tamela for rides, showed me a way to spy on those in the living room of Bellington Manor Inn, the home she grew up in. The inn is run by her son, Frank, and her daughter-in-law, Galena. They also live in the huge house and inn, only a block from my home. Charlotte was moved out to a cottage at the back of the property years ago. It's a delightful cottage, but Charlotte hates it, hates the inn, and basically hates most of life.

I doubt Galena will recognize me because she is only interested in important people. However, my spying in the inn resulted in a tussle in her backyard with one of her guests who was also her friend—and a murderer.

"Mrs. Mantelle," Charlotte barks as she hobbles with her cane to the chair across from me. "You can put your menu down. No one is looking at you."

"I've never been here. I just want to see what they have." I fold the menu and lay it down. "The scallops sound good."

Charlotte squints at me. "My daughter-in-law is out and about with one of her fancy friends who is staying at that motel of theirs. I can understand you not wanting to be remembered for having the audacity to spy on her in her own home, but she's not real good at paying attention when her rich friends are around." She picks up the lunch menu. "Lunch menu, pshaw. Means they can get away with giving you less food."

I mumble, "You showed me the holes," but Tamela clears her throat to cover my observation and taps the table with her menu before setting it down.

"It looks like a good selection and really good prices," she says. "Plus, I like how fast lunch specials usually get out of the kitchen. I'm having the scallops too."

Charlotte smirks at the person who drives her around town. Tamela never seems to get mad when the older woman baits her with insults and ugly opinions. Charlotte owns lots of property on the island, and one of those properties happens to be the house Tamela and her husband, Hert, live in. Tamela loves the house, and Charlotte hasn't raised the rent in the last five years. I've seen the house, and it's cute but...

I'm not sure it's worth it.

Annie and Cherry, whom we usually sit next to, are at the other end of the table. Lucy, our fearless leader, is out of town. I smile and wave past the half dozen or so ladies between Annie and me to make up for getting out of her car last night in such a bad mood. She grins, winks, and then makes a smooching motion at me. I turn away from her. I've got to have a serious talk with her about her insinuations about me and Charlie. I'm married. He's married. End of story.

Tuning in to the conversation going on around me, I hear Tamela say to Charlotte, "I only asked. You seemed glad to see Galena, and that surprised me."

Charlotte's smile slowly stretches, and once again she reminds me of a spider sitting in the middle of a huge web, spinning and planning traps. She's squat and wears layers of clothes even in the heat. Her hair is a solid, iron gray and cut closely around her face. Her eyes are magnified by her big glasses, which sit on the end of her nose. She scrunches her nose to move her glasses up, and she croaks, "She might have the Bellington name, but as long as I'm alive, I'm the true *Mrs.* Bellington, and it doesn't hurt to remind her. Especially in a public place with one of her la-di-da friends." With a cackle, she looks over her shoulder. "Let her explain why she's relegated her husband's mother to a shed in the backyard." She scrunches her nose again as she looks up and around the room. "Where's our waiter? Just because they're going to give us less food doesn't mean they don't have to treat us like tourists."

Tamela hisses, "Charlotte, we just got here. Our waitress is at that end of the table. They got here first."

"It's the way you drive. I didn't think we'd ever get here." She shifts around and raises her arm at the waitress who is still two people away from her. "How many crab cakes come in this lunch meal?"

The waitress lifts her head quickly and says, "One." Then she looks directly at the woman whose order she is taking. Charlotte frowns, but Tamela and I grin at each other. The waitress is in her thirties and apparently isn't someone to be bullied by a disgruntled customer. Given that Sophia Island is a tourist area, most of the waitstaff here are excellent: courteous, professional, and used to dealing with entitled diners.

She gets to us, takes Charlotte's order

with no nonsense, and gives me and Tamela a wink to let us know she knows the score. She leaves with our orders at about the same time we hear a train whistle and the bridge begins swinging into place. Everyone turns to watch; it's impressive how efficient it seems. As we turn back around, Galena and her guest come to stand at our end of the table.

Galena's brown hair is pulled back into a low ponytail. She's attractive and probably in her early fifties. "Hello. We had an early lunch as we have an appointment with a real estate agent, so we're taking our leave, but I wanted to introduce you to my friend. Catherine Forsyth, this is Jewel Mantelle. Her husband is from Sophia Island and an old friend of Frank's. Catherine, you've met Frank's mother, and this is…" She weakly waves at Tamela but doesn't wait for an answer. "Another friend." Her attention is back on me, and her friend's is as well.

Catherine nods at me. "Call me Cathy."

I smile at them. "Hello. Nice to meet you." Then I lift my hand toward Tamela. "This is my friend Tamela Stout."

Galena's eyes flit to my left as she smiles quickly. "Nice to meet you. So, Jewel, when are you and C. J. coming to dinner? We must get together. How about Friday, since

Cathy will still be here? Oh, I know!" She brightens up. "You'll come for cocktails. It's very casual. Six o'clock." She looks down and places a hand on her mother-in-law's shoulder. "Mother, you should come also." Galena laughs and looks at her friend. "We always invite her, but she's so content in her little cottage, she just won't come out."

"I'm sorry, but..." I sputter, but then Charlotte interrupts.

"I believe I will come for cocktails since my dear friend Jewel will be in attendance. We'll be there at six, won't we, Jewel?" She tips her head toward me. "Last time you were there at cocktail time, we ended up not actually *having* a cocktail, did we?" asks the spider as she spins.

My face heats up as I remember spying on Galena and Frank's cocktail hour through the little holes in the wall. "Well, Craig is out of town, and Charlotte doesn't need me—"

Cathy shakes her head quickly. She looks to be in her late forties, but she spent more time and money getting ready today than I did. Her blonde hair is shoulder-length and curled into those so-called effortless, beachy waves. They are not effortless; I've tried to do them. "Please come, Jewel. I've heard so much about you and your home. I bet it has some very interesting properties. Do you believe in the spirit world? I'm very interested in the historic homes here with spiritual activity. Have you felt, uh, movement in your house?"

Hm. I would not have pegged this woman as a ghost hunter. "No. No, I haven't."

"Ooh," Galena says. "Your house is going to be on the Christmas tour of homes, and maybe we should start a Halloween tour of homes! We can discuss it over cocktails Friday. All the idea people in town will be there."

I try to laugh, although I'd kind of forgotten the Christmas tour. That's, like, in a few months.

Mrs. Forsyth reclaims my attention as she leans forward and her eyes lock on to mine. She pleads, "Come so we can talk some more."

"Sure. Okay," I acquiesce, then look behind them. "Oh, looks like our food is here!" Maybe I said that with too much excitement, but I want out of this conversation. I thought I'd gotten used to people being excited about our house, but its spiritual activity?

Galena and Cathy smile and wave at me as they leave. Our food smells and looks delicious, and our waitress has gotten everyone's orders correct, much to Charlotte's chagrin. She even remembered the extra cocktail sauce and lemon Charlotte asked for.

Before I've tasted a scallop, Tamela says, "Well, that was weird. Galena acted almost friendly."

I shake my head as I lift a bite of perfectly grilled scallop. "Seriously? You thought Galena Bellington being friendly was the weird part?"

Charlotte slowly chews her first bite of crab cake as she stares at me. "Mark my word, Catherine Forsyth isn't moving here. Maybe they would buy a beach bungalow but why would they want another big, historic house to take care of? They already own one of the biggest and oldest homes in Buckhead. No, there's something else going on."

Tamela squeaks. "Buckhead? Oh, it's beautiful there." She looks at me, shaking her head in amazement. "It's very exclusive, and those homes are outrageous. When we lived near Atlanta, Hert and I used to drive around there just to look at the homes, at least the ones you could see from the street. The Forsyths must be rich."

Adding salt to my asparagus, I look up with a little laugh. "Is no one going to mention the ghost stuff? I thought that was really weird, but okay, whatever. Anyway, at least Mrs. Bellington doesn't seem to hold it against me. You know, the spying and all."

Striking her fork hard on her plate, Charlotte roars, "*I'm* Mrs. Bellington. She's just Frank's wife!" She slumps down in her seat and focuses on her plate, dismissing us and the rest of the restaurant.

Tamela wipes her mouth with her napkin and grins at me behind it. "Well, won't Friday night be fun for you two gals?"

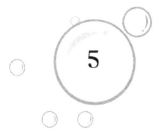

5

At lunch Charlotte went from complaining about not getting enough food to being given too much. Now Tamela is following her up the path to her cottage, carrying Charlotte's container of leftovers. I'm waiting in the car at the curb because that's what I was told to do, first by Charlotte who said I wasn't needed when I opened my door. Then, when I suggested I'd just walk home, Tamela said she wanted to ask me something, so after Charlotte got out, I took her place in the front seat.

As I look down the street, it strikes me again how dense and lush everything is here in Florida. In our historic neighborhood, trees hang heavy and low, draped with swags of Spanish moss, and the undergrowth is thick even in the tiny strips between the old houses. The streets are narrow, so that adds to the closeness, but it's more how fast everything grows. Up north, things tend to slow down after the spring and early summer sprint, but not here. Of course the daily rain showers can't help but egg on every growing thing. I'm still getting used to the heat, but all in all, I'm loving it. The people, the small town, even the heat, it all feels more like home than any other place I've lived. And my house—no, *our* house—has so much potential. So many options to consider.

Looking to the side, I study the courtyard of the Bellington Manor Inn. I've decided to start narrowing my options on what to do with the house by figuring out what I don't want to do. I don't want to open an inn or a bed-and-breakfast. I don't like the coming and going or the idea of basically being staff. But then what to do with all that space? The house and yard are both open and ready to be molded into, well, something.

Tamela catches my attention coming down the path from Charlotte's cottage. Tamela is small and walks fast. She has dark brown hair and worries a lot. Her husband's recent retirement has not helped on the worry front. Hert likes to get involved in everything Tamela is doing.

"Whew! That woman complains more than anyone I've ever seen," Tamela exclaims as she jumps in the car. "Glad I left it running. It's so hot out there. Okay, now." She turns to me and lets out a breath. "You really can't be seen around town with Charlie Greyson."

"'Seen around town'? What are you talking about?"

She holds up a hand. "I'm sorry, but you have to know. Charlie is from Sophia Beach, but so is Fiona. His wife?" Her lips settle into a firm line, and she shakes her head at me. "Everyone always said he should leave her, but no one ever thought he would. Including Fiona. She and her friends are not to be taken lightly."

"I am not going out or 'around town' with Charlie Greyson!"

She stops shaking her head and sighs with disappointment. "Out for a walk together? Then sitting in his yard in the dark?"

"Really? We just happened to run into each other. We weren't, like, *together*."

"Jewel, he likes you. Everyone can see it."

"I'm married too. We haven't done anything to be ashamed of." I try to calm my emotions by looking out the side window.

Tamela reaches over, laying her hand on my arm. "Of course not. But Fiona has never been threatened."

"And she shouldn't be now." I whip back around. "Maybe I should call and just tell her that."

"Oh, Lord, you really aren't good at this relationship stuff, are you?"

My eyes narrow. "Did Annie tell you all this?"

"Puh-lease. Annie thinks it's a big joke. People like Fiona don't bother Annie, but that's just because Annie is Annie! Between her kids and her attitude, she just blasts right on through stuff. But Fiona..." Distracted, Tamela's eyes wander behind me, and I turn to follow her look into the courtyard behind Bellington Manor. "What? What are you looking at?"

"Galena's invite today? Maybe it is all about that Forsyth woman, but, well, you don't know who Galena's best friend is, do you?"

Oh. "It's Fiona, isn't it?"

Tamela's eyes are sad even when she's happy, and they're really sad-looking now. She slowly nods.

I shift in my seat. "And you think she'll be there Friday night?"

"Probably. And as for your being out walking with Charlie, no, Annie didn't tell me first. Lucy texted me from the conference she's attending in Asheville to warn you to stay away."

"Lucy? Someone told Lucy in North Carolina?" I lay my head back against the car seat. This is too much.

"And, well…"

"There's more?"

"Fiona *might* be telling people you *might* be kind of stalking Charlie." She shrugs and frowns like she's not sure. But she's sure. "And she *might* be insinuating that's how we helped solve those murders. That you were getting information through, you know, well, spying on Charlie or, well, getting him in compromising positions where he had to talk to you." She squints as if the words hurt coming out.

They sure hurt hearing them. I close my eyes and breathe through my nose to calm down. "Okay. That's good to know. I just have to stay away from Charlie and any investigation. All this mystery stuff was never my idea anyway."

Tamela puts the car into drive. "That's a

good plan." She laughs as she pulls out of her space. "Besides, how many dead bodies can one town have?"

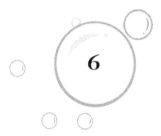

6

"I have two sons, Tibby and Finn," Cathy Forsyth tells me as we stand in the Bellington Manor Inn library, having our cocktails on Friday. Charlotte is also standing with us, but Mrs. Forsyth is ignoring her completely. Even more concerning is that Charlotte doesn't seem to mind. She's too busy listening—and watching. Cathy continues. "So you said all four of your children live out of state, but who is the young woman who lives with you? Do you know if she's sensitive to the spirits?"

"Oh, Eden Church. She's from Sophia Island, but she was looking for a place to live and I needed her help. As for spirits, I don't know."

I stop talking as Cathy's gaze wanders

around the room, and I can't help wondering if there are spirits here. I glance at Charlotte, whose eyes are focused on Cathy, but then they leap to me. She shoves her hand holding her cane at me and croaks, "You needed her help for what? Don't leave Mrs. Forsyth hanging."

"Oh, Eden knows old furniture and helped me decide what to keep, what to sell, and what to donate." The conversation stalls again, and I'm uncomfortable, but I jump in before Charlotte can give me another shove. "I hear your family owns an older home in Atlanta?"

Cathy sniffs, then takes a sip of her drink. "Yes. My husband's family is all from Georgia and the home is older, but it's dead. No activity at all. Galena says your husband is from here?"

"Not exactly. He spent summers here with his aunt years ago." I look down and notice my pinot grigio is giving me a good escape plan. "Well, my glass—"

"You said he's traveling? Does he travel often? I hope to meet him before I have to go home." As she talks, she waves at a young man hired for the party, then points to my glass. He approaches with a bottle of wine, so there goes my excuse for moving on. Last time I was here during cocktail hour there were no hired waiters, which was beneficial to spying behind the bookcase on the far wall. As folks came to fix their drinks at the small bar there, Charlotte and I could hear their conversations. Tonight must be a bigger deal than normal. There are a lot of people here. Galena did say the people in charge of the Christmas Tour of Homes would be here. If I had any idea who they were I'd avoid them, but…

I thank the waiter for refilling my glass and answer Cathy's questions about Craig. "He's working a big project in South Florida, so he's rarely here."

"That's what I've heard. Hopefully our paths will intersect." She jumps as Galena touches her back.

Our host asks, "Is everyone doing well here? Cathy, this is my friend Fiona I was telling you about."

Fiona steps into our circle with a grin as Galena tries to slide in front of her mother-in-law and exclude her from it, but Charlotte holds her ground, leaving Galena to move behind her. I wish I could slide behind Charlotte. Even without all the gossip, Fiona Greyson is one of those formidable women who makes me nervous. She's a mean girl from way back.

The two attractive, blonde women nod at each other, but then, as if they'd choreographed it, they turn in unison to me.

Fiona reaches out her hand. "Mrs. Mantelle. Do I get to meet your husband this evening? He seems rather elusive."

Charlotte laughs as she shifts to keep her daughter-in-law from entering the circle. "Oh, that C. J. is definitely a man who's hard to keep track of. So convenient, wouldn't you say, Fi? Not like when your man walks a beat and knows everyone and everything, eh, Fi?"

"Charles does not walk a beat." She reluctantly looks away from me to speak to Charlotte. "He's a sergeant, so of course he knows a lot of people." She looks confused for a moment as Charlotte's grin grows wider.

"So, Fi, how's his new house?" Charlotte's grin turns evil. "Or maybe we should ask Jewel here."

I'd just taken a swallow, a big swallow, of wine. I choke on it and start coughing. Looking apologetic, I back away, but then I'm stopped by Galena, who moves behind me and is patting my back.

"There you go," she says, still patting and not letting me leave. "Just take a big breath."

She lightly sets her arm around my shoulders, ensuring that I can't leave. "Charlie did move into our neighborhood. Only natural we'd all run into each other, right, Jewel?" When she looks around at me, her mouth is tight. "But I have to admit I've not been invited for a sunset swing."

Fiona arches one eyebrow and a flash of anger crosses her face. One look at her friends face, and Galena can't get her arm off my shoulder fast enough. Charlotte's leans toward me and I try to maneuver out of the circle.

Cathy Forsyth grasps my arm. "I think you need some water. Come with me."

She pulls me across the room and out the hall door. When we are out of sight of the library, she stops, drops my arm, and takes a deep breath. "Ignore Fiona Greyson. She seems like a wannabe, and I think she always will be." She points to a bench in the hallway. "Sit there. I'll be right back," she says as she heads down the hall toward the bright light of the kitchen. She's back quickly with a cold bottle of water.

"Thank you." I start to stand as she hands it to me, but she sits down beside me.

"Take your time. I know I, for one, am happy to be out here. Galena and I were in college together, and she's never been able to identify and avoid the mean girls." She laughs a little and then eases off her heels. "Besides, my feet are killing me. Now tell me, how do you like Sophia Island?"

It's quiet and it feels good to sit down, so I smile and answer her. "It's surprising how quickly it feels like home."

She leans back against the wall and sighs. "That sounds wonderful. I'm having trouble feeling at home in Georgia, and I believe this would be a wonderful place to end up."

"Have you been here many times?"

When the pause goes on too long, I take a closer look. Cathy's gaze is focused on the empty wall across from us. "A few times, but not recently. I remarried, and my husband sees no reason to leave Atlanta, even for a visit." She shakes herself and sits up straight. "Well, they'll be looking for us. I'll stop by your house to chat in the morning," she says brightly as she stands. "No, I know! Let's go to that darling little coffee shop on Centre Street. I'll meet you there at eight."

I follow her as she heads back toward the library. "And no telling Charlotte, Galena, or Fiona. Just us!" She grins, and holding her head high, she enters the swirl of talk, alcohol, and bodies. I hang back and watch her.

I'm not sure what to think about Cathy For-syth. One minute she's polished and put-to-gether, and then she's talking about spirits. It was off-putting that she invited herself to my house and then assumed I'd go to the coffee-house with her, but then again, she did help me escape the party and brought me water. I tend to agree with Charlotte; Cathy's not moving here. She just said her husband won't even leave Atlanta for a visit, so it can't hurt to get to know her while she's here. I just hope the Mantelle Mansion doesn't have a ghost!

The front door opens, and a young cou-ple comes in. They head straight into the par-ty. I grab the door before it closes and thank whatever part of my intuition it was that told me not to bring a purse I'd have to find to be able to leave.

I'm out of here, and I refuse to worry that not telling my hosts or Charlotte goodbye will make my manners seem woefully North-ern.

These fine people wouldn't know a man-ner if it slapped them in the face!

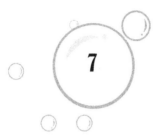

7

Eden waves me out of the line at Sophia Coffee and toward a small table in the back. When I get to it, she's there, setting the two chairs down on all four feet. "There's just two of you, right?"

"Right, but you shouldn't've saved me a table." I drop my voice to a whisper. "There's a line. I don't want you to get in trouble."

"You're the only person who doesn't expect me to save them a table, so I don't mind doing it for you. Regular coffee? I'll bring you something to eat." She turns away, but then looks back at me with an expression I can only describe as polite enforcement. "Sit down."

I take the seat facing the front of the shop so I can watch for Cathy, and I ignore the glares I'm getting from those still in the line. Annie loves this kind of special attention from Eden, but given the way things are going with Aiden, I wonder if his mother will still get treated like royalty. Aiden hasn't been around the house all week, and Eden's mood has not improved. I don't think they've officially broken up, but I'm afraid it won't be long. Because I'm avoiding eye contact with people in line, Cathy actually sees me first.

"You got a table! But what about…" Her words fade as Eden sets a mug of coffee down in front of me. My guest slips into her seat.

Eden smiles at her as she tucks a hank of her dark red hair behind her ear. "What can I get you? I know Miss Jewel only drinks regular coffee, so I didn't want her to have to wait in line for all those fancy orders, but I can make you anything from the menu."

"Oh, a regular coffee with some sweetener and just a touch of cream would be lovely." Cathy looks at me. "Should we order something to eat?"

I bite my lip and squint. "Well, Eden usually brings us things from the kitchen that they can't sell."

Cathy's eyes pop open. "Even more lovely. So you're Eden, right?"

"Yes, ma'am. We've not met, have we?"

"No, Jewel was just telling me about you last night. Sounds like you two have worked out a good living arrangement."

Eden's been more pleasant this morning than I've seen her in a while, but just at that moment, her head jerks up and she scowls as she studies the front of the shop. "I've got to go," she grunts and then flips behind the curtained door to the back.

I see the problem. Aiden has walked in the front door and is in line with another officer. I explain to Cathy, "Sorry about that, but she and her boyfriend aren't seeing eye to eye recently, and he just walked in."

Aiden waves as Cathy stretches around to look. "The young officer?"

"Yes. They hit a rough patch this summer, and I'm not sure they're going to get through it."

"Young love is difficult. But what am I saying? Old love is difficult!" she adds with a bit of a laugh.

After I nod and chuckle, I ask, "How's house hunting going? Have you seen many properties you're interested in?"

"No." Her eyes are focused on her hands, though she suddenly looks up when Eden rushes toward us, saying, "Here's your coffee and a plate of rejects. Enjoy, but I've got to get back to the kitchen."

We study the small plate of cookies and pastries, all with some small problem that makes them unsellable—a burnt end here, a poor icing job there. Cathy tears open a yellow packet of sweetener and pours a bit in before stirring her coffee. "She forgot the cream." She jumps up to get a small, disposable container off the counter, where she pauses to look up at Aiden. He nods to her and speaks, and she says something back to him before coming back to the table.

"He seems like a nice young man."

"He is. I just hope they can figure things out."

"Are they very angry with each other?"

I break off a piece of a dark breakfast bread studded with raisins, a little burnt on one edge. "They kind of are. I think some it is that they're at that age where being a kid isn't all the fun it used to be but being a full-on adult is just plain scary."

A crash near the counter jolts us, and we turn to see Aiden charging at the man behind the counter who is backing away with his hands in the air, smiling. The man looks to be in his late thirties, maybe forties, and is solidly built. "It was an accident, man. Chill out," he says, though his grin suggests whatever happened was anything but an accident.

The other officer grabs Aiden's arm and echoes the barista's comment. "He's right, Bryant. Calm down. It didn't hit you."

Aiden jerks his arm out of his co-worker's grasp. "But he did it on purpose. I've warned you, Holloway, to leave her alone."

"Eden is a grown woman. She, and everyone else, is sick and tired of you being such a little boy!" Holloway shoots back, then steps forward as Eden rushes up, also behind the counter.

"Stop it," she says. "Now what happened?"

Aiden's partner sets the broken plate, and the pieces of cake that started out on the plate, on the counter. "This fell off." He nods at Eden but then stares down the barista, who only smiles bigger and puts his arm around Eden's shoulder.

"Hon, we're fine here. You know how some guys get when they put on a badge and carry a gun. He's just trying to rattle our cage." He turns Eden back toward the kitchen, both hands squeezing her shoulders, and then he gives her a little push that direction. "I've got this." He winks at her when she looks back, then he steps to the side to pull two plates out of the display case. "Here you are, officers. Two for the price of one. Next?"

The folks in line have enjoyed the show, but they want their coffee. Aiden marches back to a table, leaving the other officer to bring the plates.

Cathy and I turn to each other and shake our heads. Well, that was ugly. I didn't see what really happened. Aiden was standing there, but I don't know how the plate ended up on the floor."

"When I went up to get the cream, he was waiting on something that was being heated. Is that big guy the owner?"

"I'm not sure who he is. I've seen him here, and I know Eden has mentioned someone named Holloway, but that's all I know."

Cathy chooses a wedding cake cookie covered in powdered sugar that has a big crack in it. "Well, he doesn't seem to like your friend Aiden very much."

"No, and I have to admit, Aiden isn't very likable lately. Like I said, I don't think he knows what he wants to do, but I think he's going to find not growing up only gets harder and harder."

"Yes, I know what you mean. My son is at that same stage. Just so disillusioned."

"You said you have two sons?"

She takes a bite, chews. "Yes. It's my old-est who seems to be stuck, but he'll figure it out. Your children are in the Midwest? That's awfully far away."

I recognize the veering conversation that means she doesn't want to talk about her children. At this moment I like all of my kids and what they're doing, so I take the passed baton and fill her in, even showing her pic-tures of my grandkids, Carter and Ellie.

Both of our coffee cups are empty before we see Eden again. As soon as Aiden and the other officer leave, she comes swerving out of the back room. "Sorry for taking so long. I was, uh, doing something important with in-ventory and stuff." Then she lowers her voice. "Did y'all see what happened up there?"

"Not really," I say. "I think I've heard you mention that guy Holloway before?"

"Yeah, he moved here last summer."

Cathy interjects. "He has a very disturbed spirit. Don't you agree?"

Eden and I both stare at her for a minute before looking at the man behind the count-er. I'd easily describe him as attractive, and the way he's smiling, it's hard to see anything disturbing about him now.

"No, not really." Eden grimaces, then

gives us a lopsided smile. "It's Aiden he has a problem with."

Cathy giggles. "I guess that comes with the territory when you're as adorable as you!"

Again Eden and I stare at her.

Eden lets out a quick breath and then waves her hand at our table. "Refills?"

Cathy puts her hand over her cup. "Oh no. Thank you, but I have an appointment. It was good to meet you, Eden. Good luck."

Eden pulls back and looks confused. "Good luck?"

I wince. "Oh, I mentioned, you know, Aiden and you."

Annoyance flashes across her face. "I need more than good luck. I need him to grow up." As she turns to go, she mutters, "Or maybe I should just grow up and forget him." Then she stomps off.

Cathy smiles. "Hope you didn't want a refill."

"No, I'm good. I need to stop by and see a friend this morning. I might as well get it over with."

Cathy stands. "That doesn't sound exactly fun."

"They're not fun people, but don't tell them that. It's actually Eden's parents. Mostly her mother. She's been kind of down lately, so I'm supposed to ask her about throwing a birthday party for Eden."

We begin walking to the front doors, where the shop has emptied out considerably. Near the front, we stop when a television hanging on the sidewall catches her attention. She points to it. "There's going to be a hurricane?"

I shake my head as I stare at the screen too. "Everyone keeps telling me to ignore it. They say they'll tell me when to worry." I bend closer to her. "But I can't help it. It's right out there!" I try to tamp down the anxiety in my voice as I point to the big, red swirl that's going around slowly, slowly, and moving even more slowly toward the coast. Sure, it's down south, but what if it speeds up? What if it speeds up at night? What if I wake up one morning and it's here?

I push open the doors and she follows. The heat pulls at my skin and hair, so I try to slow down. "Everyone says it's still a tropical storm, which they say is nothing to worry about. They're really good at ignoring it, and they say I will get that way in time, but I don't know. I mean, it is hurricane season."

Cathy's eyes mirror mine, fraught with worry, but I notice there aren't the little creases in her forehead I'm cultivating with all my watching of The Weather Channel. Either she's not a worrier or she's had Botox. She asks, "So it's hurricane season? I didn't think about that." We move on down the sidewalk.

"Yes. It started June first and goes all the way through November!"

Botox or no, there is now a definite crease as she stops in the middle of the sidewalk. "That's six months!"

"Exactly!" I huff out a huge breath. "Finally someone else who sees the problem."

She looks around and then starts walking. "I'm meeting the real estate agent at her office, which apparently is just before I get to the old post office. Galena says it's a big, white building I can't miss."

"She's right. It fills most of a block and is a couple of stories tall, with a wide staircase right off the sidewalk. All of it in white marble. I'm going in that direction, so I'll show you." We walk in silence. I hope I didn't scare her. I really didn't want to do that. I wave my hand out to my side. "I mean, all these old buildings have stood for decades, so maybe hurricanes aren't that bad here?"

She nods and speeds up. "That's probably true. Besides, Georgia is just across the river there, so maybe they're worse farther down south."

"Probably." I point ahead. "See, there's the post office. Is this your Realtor?"

Cathy checks the names on the door. "Yes. I'm going to ask her about this hurricane business. I hadn't even considered that." She leans in to give me a hug, which still surprises me when I barely know the person. But when in the South... "Thanks for meeting me for coffee. Tell Eden I said thank you for the treats. I don't think I remembered to thank her."

"I will. There's where I'm headed." I nod toward the Churches' tattoo parlor across Centre Street.

When I look back with a smile, Cathy's stepped away and is already pushing open the door.

"This heat is too much. I'll talk to you later," she says and disappears into the dark, cool office.

"Okay," I say to the closing door. At the brick crosswalk, I chuckle to myself. "Compared to her fear of hurricanes and distress at the heat, I'm practically a native Floridian."

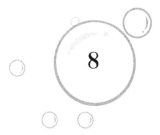

8

"I think we should have the party at my house," I say—again.

Kerry is puttering around her little kitchen in the apartment above her tattoo shop and not paying any attention to what I'm saying. Her long, curly hair is pulled back into a tight ponytail, and it hangs limp because it's obviously not been washed in a while. She's wearing an old T-shirt and baggy shorts. What she's actually doing in the kitchen I have no idea, but she's been doing it since I got here.

"Kerry. Come sit down. Let's talk." I push out the chair beside me at the small table, and she stops to stare at it. I pat the chair, and she actually walks in my direction.

She slumps into the chair and after a

moment looks at me with tears in her eyes. "I just can't get my mojo back. How could I have been so very wrong? I was fine with sending an innocent woman to jail!"

"You were *not* fine with it. We *all* thought she was guilty. She confessed. We *all* felt sorry for Victor. You have to forgive yourself and move on now. It's Eden's birthday party!"

"But what if I make that kind of mistake again? How do I ever trust my judgment?"

I'm a fairly patient person, but this is at least the sixth time she's said this. She drops her face into her hands and wags her head. I can actually smell her dirty hair. I abruptly stand up. "I can't stay here if you're going to continue to wallow in self-pity. Go volunteer at the women's shelter. Go talk to a counselor or a pastor. But at the very least go take a shower. Right now. Not later, not tonight. Now!" I grab a handful of her T-shirt sleeve, jerk her up, and pull her to the bathroom. I deposit her on the closed toilet seat and turn on the shower.

"I'm not undressing you, so you either do it and get in there or I'll be back to push you in with your clothes on. They could probably stand to be washed too!"

I stomp out and slam the door. I have to smile, though, because she was actually looking at me, dry-eyed and coherent, when I left—the first sign of life I'd seen since I got here. I make a fist and bang on the closed door. "Are you in the shower yet? Don't make me come in there!"

She screeches, "I'm in! I'm in!"

Sometimes it's good to have raised twin girls. This is not my first dirty hair pity party.

"Now for this place." It's a mess, but again, I raised four teenagers. I've seen worse.

Ted pokes his head in the door coming up the steps from the shop. "I heard the water running. Someone took a shower?" He steps into the apartment. "Hey, it looks good up here."

The bathroom door opens, and Kerry comes out wearing a big, blue robe, her hair up in a towel. Her shamed eyes jump to surprise as she looks around. "Oh, Jewel, you cleaned everything! You shouldn't've done that."

"I just kept busy waiting for you. I made a pot of coffee. We Midwesterners think everything can be solved with a pot of coffee."

Ted pats his wife's back. "Sounds good to me. Can I get you a cup, sweetie? I have to get back downstairs. We've been pretty busy today. I just heard the water running and thought I'd check." He studies her face. "So, you took a shower?"

Her shame comes flooding back, turning her face red. "Yes, finally, and it felt as good as you kept saying it would." She gives him a gentle nudge. "Get your coffee and go back to work. I'm getting dressed so Jewel and I can finalize plans for the party." She moves into their bedroom and softly closes the door.

Ted gives me a look of gratitude. "Thanks, Miss Jewel. She looks better than she has since all this started." He concentrates on pouring his coffee but says quietly, "And all this coming up again about that poor boy didn't help things."

"Oh, the one the police were checking on?"

"Yeah. I keep calling him a boy, but he was eighteen and fully able to sign the paperwork for a tattoo. Not our fault he lied, said he was healthy."

"Is that what happened?"

Ted takes a sip. "Yep. He looked perfectly healthy, and he was so excited—he wanted a shark, American traditional, right on his thigh—but he'd had heart issues since birth apparently. Not that that meant he couldn't get a tattoo, but it states right on the paper-work that a customer has to tell us."

"Did he have problems quickly?"

Ted shakes his head and starts for the door. "Not from the tattoo. It was his heart, like I told you. They first contacted us at the end of the summer when he got sick, even though all the doctors told them it had noth-ing to do with the tattoo. Then he died short-ly before Thanksgiving. The parents want someone to blame. I get it." At the door he stops and tips his head toward the bedroom. "I was really hoping no one here would ever have to hear about it. People 'round Sophia don't need another reason to get on my case. And see? I was right. It sent Kerry back over the edge when Aiden showed up asking ques-tions."

"He was just doing his job, but Eden didn't like it either. Caused problems be-tween them."

Ted grunts. "You know? It's about time they just go ahead and break up. She's just wasting her time with all this back-and-forth. Always thought she could do better." He moves on through the door, and I'm sur-prised. I've never heard anyone say that Aid-en and Eden didn't belong together. I always thought they were a great couple.

"Wait, Ted," I call before he can get down more than a couple of steps. "Do you know that guy Eden works with named Holloway? I don't remember his first name."

"Oh, yeah, it's Ron or Roy, something like that. Everyone calls him Holloway. Nice guy, why? You looking for a boy toy?" he asks, wiggling his eyebrows at me.

"What? No!"

Ted grins. "Just messing with you, Miss Jewel. Sure, I know him. Why?"

"He and Aiden got into it a bit this morning. Do you think he's interested in Eden?"

He thinks for a minute. "Wouldn't doubt it. He might be a good transition for her from Aiden. Not that he's good enough for her either."

"Do you really think she and Aiden won't work out?"

Ted leans on the stair railing. "Honestly? I don't know. They're just too comfortable. Been together since they were kids. Aiden's a mama's boy, and Eden probably needs to get off this island and spread her wings. I did, and that's how I met Kerry. Folks here think this island is the be all and end all."

He's right about that. "Okay, just wondering. You better get back to work," I say as I back away, but then his eyes crinkle into a grin.

"Listen to me. What did I do first chance I got? Scurried right back here to ol' Sophia. Just ignore me. I'm full-on garbage on most things!" He turns and trots down the steps. "Thanks again for everything!"

This island is a mix of lifelong residents and transplants like myself. I try to imagine having lived here all my life, but I can't. Maybe Eden does need to try somewhere new.

Kerry flings open her door, and she looks even more like her old self. "Whew! Sorry about all this, but I was getting plain used to feeling sorry for myself." She holds up her phone. "While I was getting dressed, I called my counselor, who also works at a women's shelter off the island, and signed me and Eden up to work tomorrow morning."

"Eden? Doesn't she usually work on Sunday mornings?"

Kerry hustles by me, headed to the kitchen. "She can take some time off to be with her mother. Besides, it's a good time, with her and Aiden breaking up, to figure out what she actually wants to do with her life. Don't you think she'd make a good counselor?"

"I guess." I've never heard Eden share any

of her career aspirations. I figured she was happy at the coffee shop. "So they've actually broken up?"

Kerry stops, coffee pot in midair. "Aiden's a nice boy, but…" She fills her cup as she wrinkles her nose. "I kind of think she needs someone older. Anyway, enough about that. Let's throw a party!"

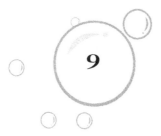

9

"I told you to stop watching that." Annie points into the living room at the muted television as she finds me in my kitchen Sunday morning before church.

"But did you see? We're in the cone now!" I'm on my third cup of coffee. It's probably not helping my nerves, which are shot from sleeping down here with the television on all night.

Just in case.

Annie folds her arms and leans back against the kitchen counter. "We live in Florida. We're practically always in the cone."

"And they upgraded it to a hurricane. And named it. Hurricane Lewis."

"Yeah? I hadn't heard that. You about ready to go?" She steps back into the living room, and I hear the television unmute. She shouts, "It's only a Category 1, so it's all good." Then she comes back into the kitchen. "Listen, did you see Eden this morning?"

I'm seated in a kitchen chair, buckling my sandals. "No. Except for last night when she was headed out at some ungodly hour. I was headed to bed, but she was going out to see a band somewhere. It was obvious she'd already been drinking." I finish with my shoes and raise my eyebrows at Annie. "I don't envy her getting up and volunteering with her mother today. They were going to serve breakfast at a soup kitchen off the island."

She sits down across from me, perched on the edge of the chair. "Aiden came dragging in this morning. Said they got into it at The Sea Snake late last night. Guess that guy she works with was there. There was also some new guy. Is she seeing someone? Do you know who it was?"

"No. She was going to meet someone, but I don't know who. I do know of a guy she works with who I think likes her. Ron Holloway, or maybe it was Roy."

Annie frowns, and I can see the name doesn't register with her, an outcome that is simply not permitted on Annie's island. "Holloway? I don't know any Holloways."

"He's in his thirties, I'd say. Works at the coffeehouse." I don't mention his dislike for her son. Sipping my coffee, I try to remember what Eden said. "I was half asleep in there watching the Channel-That-Must-Not-Be-Named when she came in. She was by herself but said she was going dancing and wanted to spruce up." I sigh. "Now that I think about it, she was dressed up more than usual when she left, and she was really excited. She had on a short skirt and a tank top with sequins on it, so maybe a guy was involved."

Annie sneers. "You know, I think I do know the coffee shop guy you're talking about. Good-looking, charming in a smarmy kind of way?"

"Bingo," I say as we both stand, and I follow Annie to the front door. "I wouldn't think Aiden would go to The Sea Snake. I mean, from what I've heard about it."

Annie harrumphs. "That's pretty much what I said this morning, and that's when he and I got into it. Again. He's just been so volatile lately." We walk down the front steps and to her car.

"So I guess he's at home sleeping it off?"

She shrugs but doesn't say anything until we get settled inside. "I don't know. I kind of kicked him out."

"Out of the house?"

She's quiet as she turns the car around. Then, as we pull out onto the street, she says, "Yeah. I didn't really mean for him to leave, but I guess that's how he took it."

We drive toward the church, and as I sneak peeks at her, I can see her eyes fill with tears. Annie may spar with her kids, but they rarely have full-on fights. I reach out and pat her arm. "I bet he'll be home waiting on the front porch for you by the time church is over."

"I don't know. He was pretty mad at me, but even more so at Eden. He can sure have a hard head when it comes to admitting he's wrong. Plus, his daddy had a fierce jealous streak, and I've been seeing it lately in Aiden as Eden and he have had trouble. I just don't know if he can let Eden go."

Annie didn't feel like going out to lunch after church, so I had her drop me off at Downtown Deli for a tuna sandwich. When one of the sidewalk tables clears, I decide to enjoy my lunch there. Watching the tourists brings back memories of summer vacations with the kids. Craig always had lots of hotel points from working out of town, so we traveled all over the Midwest and upper South, seeing local attractions and swimming in hotel pools. I always enjoyed traveling with Craig and looked forward to it with this move, but…

"Oh!" I exclaim as I think for the first time about Craig and the hurricane. Is it landing near him? Grabbing my phone and ignoring my sandwich, I call him.

Before he can say hello, I say, "Craig! Are you watching that hurricane? Is it close to you?"

He chuckles. "Hello to you too. Yes, I'm watching it, and it's still a good ways off-shore. Everyone says it's nothing to worry about yet."

I take a deep breath. "Yeah, that's what they keep saying to me too."

Silence fills the line, and I pinch off a piece of bread. "Well, sorry for bothering you, but it came to my mind and so I called you on impulse. I actually just sat down to lunch."

"Did you go to church this morning? I know you said you were going with Annie some this summer."

"I did. Her church is right downtown, and there's a lot of nice people. I see Erin's already sent her morning pictures of Ellie.

Looks like they were headed to church with her all dressed up in that frilly dress." Often Erin includes Craig and me on the same text—a little bit to save time, a little to keep us connecting, I think.

"She sure is cute." He pauses. "Um, thanks for calling, but I'll let you get back to lunch. Your friends are probably waiting."

"No, I'm eating by myself. Annie had a fight with her son, so she didn't feel like lunch."

"Her son Aiden, or the one that works at the marina—Adam, I think?"

"Aiden," I say, though I'm trying to find a way to share my surprise that he remembers their names without it sounding snotty.

He laughs. "You didn't think I remembered them, did you?"

I relax and laugh too. "Honestly? No. I mean, there are a lot of them, and with all those 'A' names."

"I've got to say I'm glad you have made good friends there. You sound, well, happy."

"I am. This place just feels right. I'm sitting outside at a little table eating by myself, and I'm enjoying it. You know how I used to hate eating by myself."

"Yeah. You'd always be so curious about how I had no problem eating most of my dinners alone on the road. Or maybe you were just jealous, seeing as you had a houseful of kids to feed."

I chuckle. "Maybe a little, but, well, you know I enjoyed being there with the kids, right?"

"I do." He pauses, then clears his throat. "I'll let you get back to your lunch. Now that you've gotten me thinking about it, I'm hungry. Been holed up in the room getting some work done, but I need to find breakfast or lunch. I have an extensive array of fast food within walking distance."

"Don't do that. Go somewhere nice. Sit down and relax."

"Maybe…"

Who am I kidding? We both know he'll end up back in the hotel with lunch in a bag and work the rest of the day. I can't help but think of how hard he worked all these years to make our lives what they were. It may be old-fashioned to think, but he sure has been a good provider, and I don't care what anyone says: that's attractive. My voice softens, and I smile at him through the phone. "Okay. Well, keep an eye on the hurricane. I'll talk to you later."

My tuna sandwich is thick, accented by crispy lettuce and ripe tomato. My tea is half sweet and half unsweet. I can't do full-on sweet tea—yet. My table is in the shade, and a breeze keeps the heat tolerable. The deli is on a side street, but there are lots of walkers and shoppers and folks out for Sunday lunch. Everyone is walking slowly, and I've noticed I walk more slowly now that I've been here for the better part of a year. That's partly from the heat, but mostly because I don't need to be anywhere at a certain time. Years of shuffling kids from one activity to another set my internal clock on high speed, but that's getting rusty, slowing down. And I'm liking it.

If Kerry was a fortune teller in another lifetime, maybe I was a Southerner.

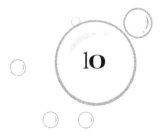

10

"So, what has to be done before the party next weekend?" I think to myself after changing out of my sundress and sandals. I've decided it's too hot to work in the yard today, plus I don't really know what to do out there, so I'm more focused on getting the inside of the house ready for Eden's party.

I haven't hung anything on the walls because I'm still undecided on the question of painting. The main living room is covered in wallpaper that is in surprisingly good shape for its age. There were a couple of places where it had come loose, but Eden watched a YouTube video, mixed up some glue, and put it all back into place. The background is cream with small, gold stripes and bunches of pale-blue flowers inside the thin, golden

columns. It's old-fashioned, but it's not awful. Besides, with these tall ceilings, I'm not
ready to paint the main room, especially not
in time for the party. Maybe I'll get a nicer
rug for the main entrance, blue to match the
wallpaper flowers, but that's it for this room.

The kitchen has tall, wooden cabinets that
aren't especially nice. We'll probably change
them out if we stay here, but they all close,
sort of, and they hold a lot of dishes and ap-
pliances. They are pretty dull, though, and
we'll be spending a lot of time in the kitchen
during the party. My to-do list gets started
as I jot down "clean cabinets." I'm planning
to paint the backsplash one day, maybe this
week? Eden and I decided a shiny white
would make it look like those subway tiles
everyone is using these days. We even already
bought the paint, so that's second on my list,
but it's only if I run out of other things to
do. As if. The walls in here will be painted
at some point, but I'm not sure on the col-
or yet, and again the high ceilings give me
pause. Right now the walls are a dingy gray,
but then again, gray is in style, so they are
what they are.

Speaking of ceilings, I crane my neck and
study the cracked paint. We're going to need
to hire someone; that's just all there is to it.

But not before the party. I lower my gaze; no point in looking up at what isn't getting done this week. Concentrating on the kitchen has me rounding out my list with things like mopping, washing windows, and bleaching the counter, which is covered in tiles. It's really not bad-looking, but the grout is stained and we've tried everything but bleach, so bleach it is.

The afternoon flies by, and soon the kitchen cabinets are actually shiny from the spray polish I applied and rubbed in. I also cleaned the backsplash and will paint it tomorrow, but I'm done working for today. Now that I've cleaned myself up, I can't wait to celebrate by starting the third book in a new mystery series I found.

The Scumble River Mysteries by Denise Swanson are set in a small town in northern Illinois, and I'm enjoying being back in the Midwest, even if only in a book. Although the series is twenty years old, I'm excited because it's a long series, so I'll get to read about Skye and Scumble River for quite a while to come.

I fix an iced coffee and settle into my lounge chair. I've muted the television, but I go ahead and turn it off. Keeping an eye on Hurricane Lewis is getting boring. He's just hanging out in the same place while the forecasters keep coming up with new ways for him to eventually travel.

My phone ringing startles me and causes me to drop my paperback. I sit forward to retrieve it while I answer Annie's call. "Hi. How's your afternoon going?"

"Better. Especially if my conjecture is correct. I've been sitting here on pins and needles waiting on Aiden to come back home, and then I realized his fishing poles are gone. Then I really got to looking, and there's a cooler missing and food, so he's gone fishing obviously, but I'm hoping he didn't go alone. The amount of food he took looks like it wasn't just for him. You ain't seen Eden, have you?"

"No, but she was volunteering with her mom this morning, so I assumed she went back to their apartment for a while."

"Or she's with Aiden."

"But I thought they fought last night."

"But what if they made up? What if they're out together right now? He did take the whole bag of ginger snaps, and those are Eden's favorites."

"I didn't know she likes ginger snaps."

"Well, she does. I mean, Aiden does too. But the whole bag?"

Annie has convinced herself of this scenario, and I know it's best to just let her have it. Besides, she's often right when she comes up with these things. She's a pretty good detective… and mom. "Well, I hope you're right. I've been cleaning and getting ready for Eden's party next Saturday. It would be great if they're back together for it."

"You know it!" she exclaims. "Look, I gotta go. Just wanted to check with you that Eden is with Aiden. Glad you haven't seen her. Talk to you later!"

I hang up and can't help shaking my head. She's practically willing the couple to work things out while Kerry and Ted are portending their end. Just as I lay the phone down, it rings again. Speak of the devil—"Hi, Kerry."

"Hi, Jewel. Sorry, but can you go wake up my daughter and tell her to turn her phone on? Just because she's out till all hours of the night causing a scene at that dive doesn't mean she gets to blow off volunteering with me and then sleep all day!"

Her lackadaisical attitude from yesterday is gone. She is fired up, and I'm just glad it's not directed at me. "Kerry, I don't think she's here. I saw her last night, but she hasn't been around all day. I mean, I haven't looked in her room, but I haven't seen or heard her either. I thought she was with you. You're sure she's not out somewhere else? Maybe with friends?"

"Out with friends? I'll accept a hangover, but I will not accept her avoiding helping with breakfast at the shelter so she can play around with her friends."

I'm not mentioning Aiden. Kerry and Ted don't see him as a good match for Eden, so Kerry wouldn't be happy with Annie's scenario. "Let me go see if she's upstairs. Hold on."

At Eden's door I knock and wait, then knock again. Then I call her name as I slowly push open the door. I look around and see the shorts and T-shirt she had on when she came in to change last night. They are laying on top of the covers, so I don't think she slept here. Which surprises me. She hasn't ever not slept here without texting me beforehand.

"Kerry, she's not here. I don't think she slept here either. The party clothes she left in aren't laying around, so…"

"So she stayed out all night, and we all know she didn't stay at Aiden's since he lives with his mother."

Chewing on my lip, I wonder if I should mention Aiden going fishing. Kerry abruptly says, "I'll make some calls. It's not like her to stay out all night." Then she pauses before quietly asking, "Is it? I mean, she's not lived with us for a while now, except for a few days earlier in the summer. But I've not exactly been myself."

"No," I confirm "It's not like her to stay out all night without letting me know. She's probably just at a girlfriend's and her phone is dead."

Kerry agrees quickly. "Yeah, I bet. Let me go and I'll talk to you later." She hangs up, and I stick my phone in my pocket.

Eden's room is down the hall from my room, which is on the front corner of the house. Eden's window faces the back of the house, and her door is right at the top of the stairs. I step over to the window and check outside, then turn and look around. There's the bed, along with a wicker chest of drawers she found in the attic, cleaned, and moved in here along with a wicker rocking chair. The wallpaper in her room is more damaged than the paper downstairs, but it's pretty with pink roses tied up in yellow and blue ribbons. It looks like a garden party with the wicker and the soft, flowered quilt she brought from home. It feels like a young lady's room. I smile, thinking of it clashing with Eden's hair, tattoos, and youthful clothes, but it's a nice juxtaposition. Closing the door behind me, I start down the stairs, wondering if I should call Annie and tell her it looks like she's right. Although, why stroke her ego? Annie's ego does fine all by itself!

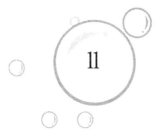

11

"I just took a chance that you were home," Cathy Forsyth says when I open my front door to the late afternoon heat. "I went out for a walk, and I found myself here. I hope I'm not bothering you."

"No. Not at all." I step back, pulling the heavy door open wider. "Come in."

She steps inside. "I don't want to interrupt your dinner or anything."

"Nothing going on. I'm just sitting here reading."

Looking around, she smiles and nods. "All by yourself? This is a nice-sized room. I like not having an entry room per se." She wanders around the living room and the rooms attached. I'm not familiar with ghost hunting, but she looks like she's hunting for something. In the middle of the side room, where I have only a couple of wing chairs, she stops, holds out her arms, closes her eyes, and turns slowly. Yep, looks like ghost hunting to me.

I watch and wait; then she drops her arms, takes a deep breath, and opens her eyes. "This is a very gentle home." Then she segues from spiritualist to real estate agent. "So many older homes are all broken up into smaller rooms, and that can be so annoying. You really have good light in here."

I laugh. "Mostly because I haven't put up curtains. When we first moved in, the bushes were so overgrown and the windows so dirty, we didn't need any coverings. Now, I'm just trying to decide how to decorate."

She stops and sighs. "But isn't that the fun part?" She's wearing long, tailored shorts in a beige linen and a short-sleeved polo shirt in navy. "Want to join me on my walk?"

"Oh, well…" I limply hold up my book. "I was reading, but…"

"Please come? The sun is heading down, and underneath the trees it's quite pleasant. Save me from going back to Galena and Frank's. I understand the cocktail hour is part of their shtick for the inn, but I just can't do it again." She reaches out and lays her hand on my arm. "Please save me."

A laugh comes to my lips, but she looks so serious. I still don't know what to think about this woman exactly, but I like her. I give her a smile and pat her hand. "Well, when you put it like that. Let me get my tennis shoes. Do you want some water?"

"I'll get it," she says as she heads into the kitchen. "This is a nice-sized kitchen," she calls back into the living room. "Another thing that can be hit-and-miss in an older home." She rejoins me as I stand up from tying my shoes. "I brought you a bottle also."

As we start out, I pause to lock the front door. "I'm assuming Eden has her keys."

"Is Eden not home?"

"No. Personally I'm wondering if she's not mad at everyone and just hiding out. She'll be home soon, I'm sure, and if she doesn't have her keys, we'll be back in a minute anyway."

We walk down the steps, headed toward the black gates at the driveway. "Which way?" she asks but then turns to the left. "Never mind, we don't want to go by Bellington Manor. We might have to join the cocktail party!"

By the time we come back around to the

corner of my property, the shadows are getting long, and we can no longer outrun the mosquitos. "Should you be getting back to the inn?" I ask.

She looks to her right, where the inn is a block away. "Actually, they were going to dinner with some friends tonight. I begged off." She starts toward my driveway, and I follow. "Besides, I don't want you to have to go into a dark house alone."

"It does look dark. I guess Eden isn't home yet." Spurred on by the bugs, we hurry up the drive and the stairs and then into the dark house. "Eden?" I call, but it's obvious the house is empty. The door was still locked.

I pull my phone from my pocket and check to make sure it's not off or something. "No messages. I'm going to call Annie and see if she's heard anything." I dial and put the phone on speaker as I enter the kitchen, Cathy following. "Annie, have you heard from Aiden or Eden?"

"No, and you know what I think? I think they've run off and eloped. I'm going to kill that boy!"

"What?" I'm pulling cheese and grapes out of the fridge, but her statement stops me. "Why would you think that?"

"Well, where else would they be? I drove

by your house and saw it was all dark. You down at Charlie's a-swinging?" she says with a loud cackle.

"No!" I roll my eyes at Cathy, who grins. "Cathy Forsyth and I went for a walk. Ended up being a long walk. Listen, let me know if you hear anything, okay? This just isn't like Eden."

"Unless she's off getting married!"

"Annie, she's not off getting married. Now call me, okay?"

"Okay. Bye."

Cathy wanders around the kitchen. She's smiling to herself, then turns to me. "So Eden's off getting married? It's not often you get such an agreeable mother-in-law. Eden's a lucky girl."

I sit two boxes of crackers on the island. "I guess you could look at it that way. Here's what I was planning on for dinner tonight. You're welcome to join me."

"Sounds like a great idea. Maybe a glass of wine? That bottle in the fridge looks perfect to me. I'm surprised how calm this house is. It really has no distressing vibes at all. It's very peaceful. That's rare. "

"Good to know. Um, I'll get the wine glasses."

"So," Cathy edges gingerly into the question I should've guessed was coming, but this lady is all over the board. She's keeping me on my toes. "I'm thinking the Charlie she mentioned is Charlie Greyson?"

"Yes, but there's nothing going on. She's just got romance on the brain. As you can tell by her thinking that Eden and Aiden eloped."

"Well, she's not the only one thinking that way concerning you and Charlie. Fiona Greyson has it out for you, and she can really be, well, not nice. She is the opposite of calm and peaceful."

"So you've gotten to know Fiona better since Friday night?" I focus on putting crackers and cheese on my plate.

"Some, but mainly, I just run in circles with a lot of Fionas." She quirks an eyebrow. "They may not want their husband, but they don't want anyone else to have him either."

"I don't want Charlie except as a friend." As I say this, there's a loud knocking on the front door, and we hear a man calling my name. We hurry in that direction, and I pull open the door as I grimace. "Hi, Charlie. This is Cathy. What can I do for you?" I'm glad I didn't turn on a lot of lights because I know my face is bright red.

His eyes shift from me to Cathy. He nods

at her and mumbles that he's pleased to meet her. Then he motions for me to step onto the porch.

I smile back at Cathy. "Go fix your plate. I'll be right in." She winks at me and turns back toward the kitchen.

Charlie motions toward his SUV in the drive. "I've got a problem."

"What kind of a problem?"

"Aiden Bryant is drunk and passed out in the back seat there."

"What? Annie said he was out fishing."

"And he might've been, but he ended up back out at The Sea Snake and caused a scene. Which apparently he did last night as well. Last night his buddies carted him out of there and took him home. Today he was by himself when he showed up, already drunk and looking for a fight. There were a bunch of bikers who didn't take kindly to his insults. The owner called me instead of calling the station, so now..." He shrugs at me. "Is Eden here?"

"No. I kind of thought she was with him."

He shrugs again and sticks his hands in his front pockets. "Before he passed out, he just kept saying he needed to tell Eden he's sorry, seemed pretty upset that he'd, I don't know, hurt her feelings or something? So I wanted to make sure she was okay."

My stomach flips. "Maybe I should call Kerry and see if she's seen her. Kerry called me earlier looking for her. What are you going to do with Aiden?"

He cocks an eyebrow at me. "What do you think? I'm taking him to his mother's. Annie Bryant is more than capable of handling this. But when he sobers up, he's going to be in trouble with me. Serious trouble. I'm not having this kind of behavior in one of my officers." He jogs down the steps, saying behind him, "Let me know what Ted and Kerry say."

Cathy pulls open the door behind me as the SUV pulls out. "That doesn't sound good. I hope Eden is okay."

"Me too," I say as I step inside and dial Kerry, praying under my breath, "Please let Eden be there."

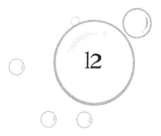

12

"If he laid one hand on my baby, I'll kill him," Kerry says again. Just not as loud this time, as I've managed to get her to sit down on the couch and Cathy has put a glass of wine in her hand. When I called her, she had already heard of Aiden's antics at The Sea Snake, and she and Ted were on their way here. Luckily, Charlie with his snoring cargo was long gone.

Ted is pacing and keeping his phone hot. At this point the entire island has to know Eden is missing and Aiden is to blame because that is exactly what Ted has blasted on every local Facebook group he can find. In between his postings, he's calling anyone he can think of and has even organized search groups. When asked where they should be searching, he was rather vague, but he's put it out there to look wherever Aiden Bryant likes to fish, to look into all the downtown and beach area bars, and, well, anywhere Eden has ever been. It's not a really organized search, but he sure has made Aiden look guilty.

My phone rings, and it's Charlie, so I quickly get to the back office and close the door. "Charlie. This is a mess. Ted and Kerry are beside themselves. You don't think Aiden could've hurt Eden, do you?"

"Not intentionally, I don't. However, accidents happen, and he's not helping himself by apologizing for whatever he did do so publicly at The Sea Snake. And brace yourself: There's video of him out there this afternoon. He's real sloppy drunk and talking about Eden and some other guy. I'm trying to keep the local groups from posting it, but some of them just don't care, so I figure it'll be out any minute. Ted sure is stirring up a hornet's nest, but I did learn where Aiden was fishing this afternoon, so I'm headed out there with a couple of other officers. Keep Ted and Kerry there, and for God's sake, take away his phone!"

He hangs up, and I stare at my phone,

shaking my head. "Yeah, like that's going to happen."

Cathy is just outside the door to the office and jumps as I pull it open. "Oh, there you are. Are you okay?" she asks.

"I'm fine. Thanks for being here, but you don't have to stay. This is all kinds of crazy."

"Oh, I'm happy to help. I put out the rest of the crackers and cheese. Probably good for them to eat something. Could be a long night." We walk into the living room as she says, "You know, police officers have been under a lot of scrutiny lately. Maybe he just snapped."

Kerry gasps. "That's right! Maybe he just snapped."

"No, that doesn't sound like him at all," I say. "Cathy, you don't know Aiden. He loves Eden. Kerry, you know he loves her. You know him. We just need to calm down."

Ted groans and sits down on a chair beside the front door. "Why did we let her date him for so long? We knew it was trouble. And his cop friends will cover for him. You know they will!"

I turn on him. "Ted, what are you saying? I just had dinner a few weeks ago at your home with Eden and Aiden. You all were fine. He's a good guy, you know that."

I can't believe how quickly this is all unravel-
ing. "Cathy, I don't think she needs any more
wine," I say when I see her refilling Kerry's
glass.

Cathy nods and pulls back the bottle, but
the glass is already full.

I sit beside Kerry and get her to look
at me. "Listen, Eden is probably just off
thinking things through. We shouldn't get
so worked up. Charlie is taking control of
things now."

Ted stands up. "I'm going out to look
around. Can't just sit here like this. Some of
the guys are coming to pick me up. Kerry,
you stay here."

She jumps up off the couch. "Maybe I
don't want to stay here."

Cathy pats Kerry's back. "You need to be
around people in case you get bad news."

Through gritted teeth, I growl at her.
"Cathy." Then I pull on Kerry's arm. "Go upstairs and check Eden's room. Maybe you can
find something that tells us where she is. A
new girlfriend's number, anything like that."

She nods at me and is halfway up the
stairs when Cathy says, "I'll go with her."

Ted groans again at his phone and then
reels off into the kitchen.

I hurry after him, afraid the video has made its appearance. "What is it?"

"Look at this. Kerry can't see this. It'll kill her." He holds his phone out, and I see that he's watching a dark video of several guys. There's a lot of jostling and cursing, but then Aiden's voice comes out and he's shouting, "Do you know? Do you know?" The other guys laugh. One shoves him and he falls, but as he does, he yells, "I didn't mean it! I love her." Then he starts sobbing like his heart is breaking. The video fades as the door is opened and light floods the place. The last thing I can hear is one of the men saying something about how someone should call the police because the guy has blood on his shirt.

"Oh, that *is* awful," I say as I keep hold of Ted's phone and guide him to sit at the kitchen table. "Sit there and let me get you some water. Or coffee? I'll make you a cup of coffee." At the counter I shove his phone in a drawer. "Those kinds of videos can be deceiving. Let's let Sergeant Greyson handle things, and I bet before you know it Eden will be here and we can all get a good night's sleep."

I get him his coffee. He seems to be in shock, so I just let him sit. I step into the hall and call Cherry, my nurse friend who not only has all the info on what's going on at the hospital but will know how to help Ted.

"Hey, I've heard about Eden and Aiden. What in the world is going on? Lots of ugly rumors over here," she whispers.

"I don't know exactly, but are you still on duty? I know you work Sundays at the hospital."

"I am, but it's really quiet here, so if you need me, I can leave early."

"Could you? Ted and Kerry are here, and they are beside themselves. I don't know what to do."

"Sure. I'll be right there."

"Hello?" I hear from the living room as I hang up. Then Tamela comes around the corner.

"Hi there," she says. "We're not going to stay. Matter of fact, I made Hert stay in the car. Here's a cake."

She's got a white frosted cake with colorful sprinkles on top. "The center may still be a little frozen as I just pulled the layers out of the freezer, whipped up a quick frosting, and slapped it on. The sprinkles may be a bit much, but Hert did that while I got dressed. He never has liked an undecorated cake."

My mouth is hanging open, and I can't wrap my head around the fact that my friend showed up suddenly at this time of emergency with a cake, a homemade cake with homemade frosting. And sprinkles. "It looks good," I finally dribble out.

She leans in to give me a quick hug, pulls back, and then shrugs. "I don't know if this was right to do. I mean, that's just what my momma always did when folks were hurting." I continue to stare, and she lowers her eyes. "Sorry, I—"

But Ted interrupts her. "Cake would be good with my coffee. Ya gotta fork, Jewel?"

I pull open the drawer beside me and hand him a fork. I mean, it's better than handing him his phone.

Maybe Tamela's mother knew what she was talking about.

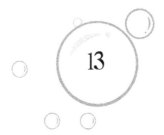

13

"Ted, there's nothing I can charge him with," Charlie says in a firmer voice this time as he leans on my kitchen table. Kerry is still upstairs where she slept last night.

It's a gray morning, and even though the early light isn't harsh, it doesn't help any of us look better. Kerry refused to leave Eden's room last night. Cherry brought over some protein drinks and got Kerry to drink one, but Kerry just wanted to be left alone, well, except for Cathy. I suspect this has something to do with Cathy's talk of calming spirits in the house and trying to connect with Eden through the spirit world. That was right up Kerry's alley, but if it helps, I'm not complaining.

Cathy was a trouper and agreed to stay

with her, so Frank brought her overnight case from her room at the inn, as well as a bag Galena packed for her. He also brought a breakfast casserole, which is warming in the oven now. He said it's what they serve at the inn and that they always have them in the freezer. I'm discovering these people keep more in their freezers than pizza and ice.

Since Kerry was staying, Ted decided to stay here too. Besides, it took him a while to find his phone. He'd gone to their apartment, backtracked everywhere that he'd walked in the neighborhood, and then scoured the house. Finally, around nine last night, I laid it under a newspaper on the kitchen counter where he discovered it, but the time away from it did him good. Then the time it took him to catch up on Facebook was calming for all of us—or maybe it was the sprinkle cake.

There's been no word, but Aiden has sobered up and Charlie came over early this morning to tell us that the young man's story matches up with what he's found so far. "I went down to where Aiden fished yesterday afternoon. His cooler and rods were there, but there was no evidence of anyone else being there."

"He's a cop. Of course he would know how to cover it up," Ted says.

"Not with all the beer he put away. Plus, he knew enough to not drive. He called a buddy to pick him up and take him to The Sea Snake. The buddy said he didn't see Eden there. He said Aiden kept saying that she wouldn't talk to him. That she wouldn't answer her phone."

I interject. "So, where was this buddy when he started falling down and insulting the other patrons and you had to be called?"

Charlie winces as he sits on the edge of a kitchen chair. "On duty. He's another one of my officers. He was on duty when Aiden called him, and I'm glad he picked him up, but why didn't he take him home? Why would he take him to a bar?" He frowns and shakes his head. "He says he just did what Aiden asked. Said Aiden told him Eden's new guy hangs out there. Then he got a call over his radio, and he was in a hurry. Plus, I'm sure he couldn't get Aiden out of his cruiser fast enough. Believe me, though: there will be consequences."

Ted jumps up and paces the room. "Right. Consequences. For the police. Don't make me laugh."

Charlie tightens his jaw. "Ted. Cut it out.

I say there will be consequences, there will be consequences. I admit we've apparently let things slip, but right now we have to work together to find Eden. Now, is she seeing a new guy?"

"I sure hope so!" he exclaims, then draws in a deep breath. "Okay. You're right. We've both gotten too comfortable in our town. Things need to be shaken up. You can bet I'll be all over that station when we get Eden back, keeping your toes to the fire, Charlie."

"That's a deal. Now, a new guy?" He looks at me. "You think you could go get Kerry?"

"She's coming right now," Cathy says as she enters the kitchen. "Good morning."

Charlie quickly stands. "Mrs. Forsyth. You're here early."

"I stayed the night with Mrs. Church. She asked me to, and how could I say no?"

Charlie's eyes find me, and I nod. Cathy pats Ted's back. "I hope you got some sleep. Your poor wife didn't have a good night." She heads to the coffee maker. "Can I get anyone a cup of coffee? That casserole smells good. Maybe we can get Kerry to eat something. She seems rather weak."

"No, I don't want anything to eat." Kerry appears around the corner, leaning against the doorframe. "I want to know what happened to my daughter. She's too young, just too young to be gone."

We all jump to deny her claim. Charlie reaches out to hold her arm, focusing his eyes on hers although she won't look up at him. "Kerry, listen to me. There is no evidence anything has happened to Eden. Right now it's entirely possible she's just off somewhere needing some time to think."

Kerry shakes her head. "No. I highly doubt that. She's not like that, and well, what about the blood on Aiden?" She looks at him, and her eyes blaze. "Are you trying to cover that up? Aiden has my daughter's blood all over him, and you're here trying to tell me she's run away."

Cathy sighs. "She found the video. I couldn't stop her."

Ted goes to hug his wife. "Sweetie, there's more of the video that explains the guy was talking about the waiter. And it wasn't blood; it was ketchup. When you watch the whole thing, it makes sense. Whoever edited that first one that came out made it look bad."

She pulls back and stares at him. Then she looks at Cathy. "They're not telling me the truth, are they? I can feel that she's gone. I can feel it right here." She puts her hand on her heart and then moans and stumbles out of Ted's arms into the living room.

Cathy waves her hand at me, saying, "I'll get her to lie down on the couch."

Ted slumps back into the kitchen chair. "Maybe she's right."

Charlie grasps Ted's upper arm. "No. We're not going to give up without a reason to give up. Right now we have a grown woman to find. The social media attention means we're already all over this. Other departments are looking, and we're going to find her. But I do need to know anything you know about this guy she was with Saturday night at The Sea Snake. As far as we can tell, that's the last time anyone saw her."

"Saturday night?" I gasp. "No one saw her at all yesterday?"

Charlie shakes his head. "We have her at the disturbance Saturday night when Aiden showed up. Lots of folks saw her and then nothing. We know she arrived alone in her car, and we assume that's how she left. But no one knows for sure. We haven't seen her car, though we have everyone looking for it. So, again, that might be a good thing if she did just decide she needed some time away."

The idea that Eden's actually been missing since Saturday night hits me hard. That's two nights. I wander through the back kitchen door, down the hall, and into the living room. Cathy has her arm around Kerry and is whispering to her. I go in and sit on her other side.

Kerry moans and leans in to me. "Can I stay here today? I can feel her presence here better than at our apartment. We sold her childhood home. That apartment was never truly home for her." She reaches over and grasps Cathy's hand. "It's important for me to remember her, isn't it?"

Cathy's wide eyes look at me, and we both sigh. I whisper, "Whatever you want is fine with me. But listen, do you know anything about a new man Eden might have been seeing?"

Her whole body shakes, and she moans. "I wish! She was through with Aiden Bryant, and he just wouldn't accept it. He couldn't let her go. So now no one can have her, right?"

Sadness fills Cathy's face. "Oh, I don't know. Let's not think about that right now. Do you think you can eat anything?"

"I don't know. Maybe I could go back upstairs and lie down? Jewel, would you tell Ted and Officer Greyson I want to go lie down? Cathy will go with me."

She struggles to get up with my help and

Cathy's, and they start up the stairs. Cathy looks back at me and shrugs. Kerry is a handful when she's feeling good, so maybe it's good someone new is around to help her right now. We all care about her, but Kerry Church's worn everyone else out this summer.

Before I get up, the two men come back into the living room and I give them Kerry's message. Ted nods, then says he's going home to shower and change but that he'll come back later since Kerry's staying.

"I'll walk out with you," Charlie says, but before he heads to the door, he nods up the stairs. "Did Kerry know this Forsyth woman before?"

"No. It's like she was just in the right spot at the right time. She speaks Kerry's language, you know, spirits and such. Plus, Kerry is pretty needy on a good day, and Cathy seems to like being needed. Maybe we're using her, but she sure is helping me out."

He grunts, then turns to the door, but I stop him. "Listen. About Eden having a new guy. There's this guy she works with. Holloway, I'm not sure about his first name. She said he moved here last summer. He and Aiden got into it Friday morning at the coffee shop. He strikes me as a charmer—

good-looking and protective, but still, something didn't sit right. He did seem to have an unhealthy interest in Eden, and he does not like Aiden. Even mentioned she shouldn't be with him."

Charlie thinks for a moment. "Big guy? Good-looking and friendly? I think he works the counter?"

"That's him. I'd never paid attention to him until Aiden's plate got knocked off the counter. I don't know, but I think he might've done it intentionally. To get Aiden upset." I shrug. "And it worked. The other officer had to hold Aiden back."

He groans, closes his eyes, and shakes his head. "In uniform, too, I bet. Ted's right to a point. We've gotten too lackadaisical." He runs his tongue across his bottom lip. "That's changing. Johnson doesn't care, but I'm through waiting on him to do something. Listen, I'll go talk to this Holloway. Check him out." He looks around the quiet house. "Coast is clear for a bit. Might be a good time for you to reach out to Annie. I told her you'd call her when you had a chance."

"Good idea. She's got to be reeling."

"I'm sure," he says and then closes the door, just as the oven buzzer says the casserole is ready.

I think I'll run some of it over to Annie's. She's so good at giving out hugs, and I bet she could use one right about now.

See? There have got to be some Southern ancestors hiding in my genealogy.

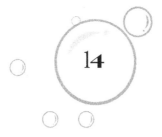

14

"Annabelle, I'm just not sure that's a good idea." I fold my cloth napkin in smaller and smaller triangles on Annie's table as her youngest, Annabelle, explains how her television station wants to have Kerry and Ted make a plea for Eden's return. I try to explain, but I don't want to be mean. "They are both pretty hard to, well, control in a *good* situation."

Annie reaches over and pats my hand. "That's what I was thinking, but what if it helps get her to come back? I mean, surely she couldn't stay away if she knew how badly her parents are doing?"

"True." I squint and look around the table. "Do the rest of you think she's just staying away?" By the time I got to Annie's, the rest of the ladies were there: Cherry, looking more rested than usual on a Monday morning, since she'd left work early last night; Lucy, back from her conference in North Carolina and ready for a morning on the courts in her cute, white tennis outfit; and Tamela, who showed up with another cake—sans sprinkles.

The three of them look at each other, making undecided noises, but they avoid looking at me or Annie. Finally, Lucy speaks up. "No. I don't. I'm sorry, I know that hurts, but I just don't see it. Eden is the very opposite of selfish. She's more the parent in her family than Ted or Kerry. As a parent, would any of you worry your children this way? No. I believe someone took her from The Sea Snake."

As I look at the faces around the table, my heart sinks, but it sinks into truth. That feels right. Annie's breath catches, and then she shudders. She feels the truth of it too.

With a nod, I tell Annabelle, "I'll talk to them. How long would it take to set it up?"

A spark leaps into the pretty blonde's eyes. "Not long at all. The crew is already here on Sophia. They're down at the police station. A young woman going missing from such a popular tourist spot as Sophia Island is newsworthy. Should I have them come to your house?"

"Oh, no. Let's do it at the station, okay?" I stand up and ask the other ladies, "So, what are you guys going to do now?"

Lucy rolls her eyes. "Well, I never thought you'd hear me say this, but I'm thinking we should go to The Sea Snake and see what they serve for lunch."

I drive home on A1A on autopilot, trying not to think. Just look out the windshield and drive.

I'd never imagined a place where the heat doesn't abate at night. Where the air conditioner is needed at all hours. Everything feels baked, even though there is almost daily rain. Heavy rain. Soaking rain, except everything it soaks is dry in less than an hour. Another thing: There are no puddles. No mud. It pours, water standing all around, and then it's just gone. Gone. But even though everything feels baked, it's so lush. And so hot.

Yet I'm so cold. Inside my bones are frozen. Lucy's right. I know Eden isn't off somewhere hiding. I want it to be true, but there's no way. Annie said Aiden has said that from the beginning, when he couldn't reach her.

That Eden was with that guy she went to meet at The Sea Snake and he hadn't liked him from the minute he saw him. Of course he didn't like him, the guy was with his girlfriend, but maybe he picked up another vibe. Something a police officer would pick up on.

Poor Eden. Annie was like me, just trying to hold out hope for an easy, happy ending. I didn't tell my friends how Ted and Kerry feel about Aiden, but I probably should give Charlie a heads-up since Aiden's at the station, which is where I'm supposed to get Eden's parents to go for their news conference.

I pull over at the entrance to the state park on the north end of the island, and I call Charlie.

"Jewel, you hear anything?" he answers.

"No, except she didn't leave on her own, did she?"

I hear him mumble something, and after a pause, he comes back on the phone. "Listen, we're working on it. I'm down at the station now, and it sounds like you're going to get the Churches to make a statement?"

"I'm going to try. But they do not need to run into Aiden. Annie says he's there?"

"Yeah. I've got him looking at pictures. See if we can figure out who this guy was.

You didn't have any idea who she was going out to see when she left? She didn't say anything?"

"I've been trying to remember, but it was so quick and I was sleepy." I sigh. "I was so hoping…"

"I know. I've gotta go."

We hang up, and I drive home. There are a couple of additional cars in the drive, so I pull around to the back of the house. The row of palm trees on the left side of the drive keeps the cars in a line, but no mud or puddles means driving in the yard isn't a problem. I try the back door and find it unlocked. I take the hallway leading between the office and the downstairs bedroom, then past the bathroom and laundry room, before I get to the rear door into the kitchen. I pause there to figure out who the voices in the living room belong to, but the only one I recognize is Ted's, and it sounds like he's on the phone. I duck into the kitchen and am astonished at the array of food on the island. Every inch is covered with dishes. Aluminum foil, plastic wrap, and dish towels cover it all, with spoon handles sticking up like battle flags. I move through the other kitchen door into the living room and right into Ted Church.

"There you are!" Ted exclaims. "We're

supposed to be headed to the police station, and you're off running around who knows where." He yells toward the stairs, "Kerry! Let's go!"

I step back to let him past, but I can't help my mouth hanging open at his anger. Galena Bellington notices as she steps to me. "Poor Ted. You have to forgive him. We weren't thinking and had the news on. They didn't say it about Eden, but they were doing a big report on human trafficking in Florida. Did you know we're the third highest state for it?" She presses her hand to her throat. "It was just awful. Those poor girls."

"Human trafficking? Here? I mean, I guess—" My mind is reeling. I've seen the stories and the movies but I can't imagine it happening here.

Galena gives me a quick hug. "You poor thing! Bless all y'all's hearts, this is just awful. Of course I contacted our church for food. Seems like they, the Churches, don't actually attend one, but of course everyone wants to help. What's the latest? We all just want to help."

From the couch I hear a little laugh, and I look past Galena to see Fiona Greyson as comfortable as can be sitting there. She smirks and acidly asks, "Yes, what is the latest? We know my husband keeps you informed of everything the police know. His superiors can't be happy with the little arrangement you two have, but he is a grown man." She stands and smooths her slim, gray skirt. "So, what is the latest?"

The bile rising in my stomach from the thought of Eden being taken by such awful people is pushed back down by the flush of cold anger at Fiona's words. Then I hear my name shrieked from upstairs. "Jewel! You're back." Kerry comes down the stairs in a hurry. "Did they find her? Were you down at the river? Are they dragging the river?"

I rush to meet her at the bottom of the staircase. "No! Why would you think that?" Cathy hurries down right behind her, and I meet her eyes.

She just shakes her head and frowns. "I might've said something about water, a feeling of water. I meant in a clean, pure way, but I guess that's not how Kerry took it."

Kerry hugs me, and over her shoulder I glare at Cathy. The tired blonde lifts her shoulders in apology. I roll my eyes at her, pull back, and ask Kerry, "Did you eat something?"

Cathy says, "I tried, but she just wouldn't."

"No. I don't need anything to eat.

Where's Ted. Ted?" She moves past me in a hurry, which seems completely odd since this morning she was moving like a sloth.

I follow her into the kitchen. "Let me make you something quick to eat. You have to keep up your strength."

"Oh, let me." Cathy grabs the plate out of my hand, then looks at me. "Shouldn't you change?"

I look down at the shorts and shirt I'd thrown on this morning. A quick look around tells me I'm definitely underdressed. "You are all so dressed up."

Galena sadly pats me on the shoulder. "It's just how we pay respects around here." She has on a brown dress with low heels, but still, they're heels. Fiona smirks with her hands on her hips, which are covered by the gray skirt. Her sleeveless sweater is also gray with flat-silver buttons. Cathy has obviously been brought a change of clothing, and she has on a dark-red sun dress with matching sandals. Even Kerry has on a black, gauzy dress with one of Eden's embroidered scarfs around her neck.

"Go on," Galena says. "We'll get Kerry to eat something while you get dressed."

I move past them and up the stairs, but

something doesn't feel right. Standing in front of my closet, it hits me.

They're dressed like we're going to a funeral.

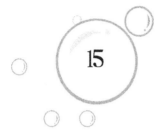

15

"This is a circus. Who let all these people in here?" Charlie growls as he strides in the side door to the conference room where the TV crews are set up. Annabelle's station isn't the only one here, and there are lots of other folks with notepads in the front row that look like they might be with newspapers. Standing to the side of the table with the microphones are the city commissioners; well, at least that's who some of them are. Public officials never seem to be in short supply when television cameras are around—and they're not in trouble.

The rest of us are smushed in the back against the closed double doors, which keep opening to let just one more person squeeze in until we're packed like sardines. We all dip our heads as Charlie scans the room because none of us wants to leave. Morbid? Probably. Leaving? No.

I mean, I have to stay to keep Annie back here away from Kerry and Ted. I should've told her they aren't Aiden's and his family's biggest fans right now, but wouldn't you think she'd have figured that out? I know; of course not. She's Annie. Everybody loves her—just ask her.

Finally Charlie throws up his hands and turns around to where the Churches are sitting with Detective Johnson. From what I know of the domineering lead detective, no one is surprised he's getting on camera. Charlie leans on the table and talks to the three seated there.

I'm keeping my head down by reading my phone, but I'm having trouble keeping quiet and not laughing out loud. Lucy, Cherry, and Tamela did go to The Sea Snake for lunch. Their running text commentary is hilarious, beginning with the decision that it smells like a frat house, which brought back good memories for Lucy and led to a text discussion of Greek life. Then came Tamela's discussion with the bartender on the pros and cons of draft beer. Then Cherry ran into a guy she knows from the hospital. She says

HIPAA regulations won't let her put down in writing what he was doing at the hospital, but it's a story for another time. Lucy then lamented that her white tennis skirt would never be the same made me choke just imagining the scene. All in all, it's been very entertaining, but they learned nothing about the guy Eden was with. I didn't add to the text stream at all because I was afraid I would say the words rocketing around inside my head—human trafficking. Google confirmed Galena's statistics about the state of Florida, which is only surpassed by California and Texas. I swallow all that and try to put it out of my head.

Annie was left off the text thread because we weren't sure what we might find out about Aiden. As I put my phone in my purse, I nudge her. "Wait'll you hear about the girls' trip to The Sea Snake."

"Shhh," she says. "It's starting. Tell me later."

Everyone looks to be in position, and the camera lights are on. Detective Johnson waves Charlie away and gives the television folks the roll sign.

Kerry and Ted say the expected words, both looking smaller than they usually do. I think it's sinking in that no one is treating this like a runaway situation anymore. The circus, as Charlie called it, devolves into silence. No one is moving as we listen, and it's as if we've all stopped breathing. Detective Johnson does a good job—I'm surprised—of presenting the facts and being compassionate. Then he clears his throat and glances over at Charlie. "We've just received a video of who we believe might have been the last person to see Miss Church Saturday night. We'll show it here on the screen, but we'll also provide the stations with the footage." That causes a bit of a stir, but we quiet down as a still clip appears. He turns to the screen. "We believe the gentleman, whom you will see in a minute, captured in this video is who we are looking for. It's short, so we'll play it a couple of times, and we've muted it to make it less confusing as nothing is said by, or about, the man in question. We'll freeze it at the person of interest. Turn the lights down, please."

The still shot is of a singer who looks to be taking a bow. When Johnson presses play, the singer finishes his bow, steps off the foot-high stage, and heads toward the camera. Then he suddenly turns to the right. As he leaves the screen, there's a man walking away from the camera, and that's when the video stops. "This is the man believed to have been with Miss Church Saturday night at The Sea Snake."

It's the man's back. It's dark in the bar, and his shirt is dark. It looks like he has longer hair, as something is hanging down to the neck of the back of his shirt, where some skin can be seen. The side of his face is visible, but none of his features are. The video goes back into motion, and he walks away, then dips his head as he walks through a doorway. There's a gasp, and I look to see if it's Kerry realizing Annie is beside me, but she has her head down on the table. When I look back at the screen, the video has started over. We watch it a couple more times, but then the reporters get restless. The lights come back up in the room.

Detective Johnson addresses the reporters. "We won't be taking questions at this time. I'll be getting the video and the man's description to you out at the front desk. Thank you." He directs Kerry and Ted to stand up, and then he bustles them out the side door to the front hall. The reporters shout their questions anyway, and Annie grips my arm when she hears the word "trafficking." We both are stunned when one shouts a question about blood found in the parking lot of The

Sea Snake. The uproar that causes among the news teams threatens to take the roof off the place. It also allows Detective Johnson and the Churches to get out of the room.

The reporters push us aside in their hurry to get to the front desk, so Annie and I scoot around the edge of the chairs and claim a couple of them while the stampede moves on.

She sighs as she sits. "This is just awful. I've seen this kind of thing on the TV before, but not when it's someone I know. Someone I love." She shakes her head briskly. "But did you hear them mention trafficking when they shouted out those questions? That's just unthinkable. Unbearable. As for there being blood, well, I just can't."

"I know. I'm so afraid for her. I can't imagine what Kerry and Ted are going through."

"They are lucky to have you. I can't breathe even imagining some stranger taking Annabelle like that. Just hauling her off to God-knows-where." She wipes her eyes, and before I can stop her, Annie jumps up, barrels across to the double doors, and marches through them. She's at the edge of the small crowd when I catch up to her. The reporters are packing up. Detective Johnson has his head bent near Ted's. Kerry is staring off into space. Unluckily the space she's staring into is the same space where Annie has stopped. Annie waves, then pushes through the chatting reporters. "Kerry, sweetie, is there anything we can do? Aiden is just beside himself, as am I. We—"

"What are you doing here?" Kerry screeches. "Your son should be behind bars! What did he do with my little girl?"

The reporters suddenly are back in action, no longer talking to their stations or writing their stories, and I see red lights on cameras flashing on as I hurry to grab Annie's arm. "Annie, this isn't a good idea." But one tug on her arm tells me she's not going anywhere. She's like a statue. A talking statue.

"He just tried to love her. That's all! She's the one that was out with another man at all hours of the night!"

Kerry darts in our direction with Ted and the detective playing catch up. "And he couldn't stand it! He couldn't just let her go, could he? He thought she belonged to him!"

Annie's mouth is hanging open, and I can see she's putting together what Kerry is saying. "You think my son hurt her? You think Aiden did this? He's a police officer!"

"Exactly!" Kerry spits, but then Detective

Johnson is between them and Ted has his arms around his wife.

The detective takes hold of Annie's arm and pulls her with him back into the room we just left. I hear him murmuring in her ear, "This will not help Aiden's case at all."

I rush toward Kerry. Ted is talking to her, close to her ear but Cathy Forsyth somehow beats me to her side. Cathy sadly shakes her head at me and whispers, "Maybe you're not the person she wants to talk to right now. You know, it looks like you're with Aiden's mother."

Stepping back, I look around at the reporters, who are both trying to get to the Churches and trying to get back into the conference room where Annie is. If Charlie thought it was a circus earlier, wait until he sees this.

Suddenly he and a couple of other uniformed officers storm into the open area. The two younger men corral the press and herd them toward the front doors. Charlie talks to Ted, and he begins walking Eden's parents back toward another door. He gives me a nod and a bit of a sad smile. I mimic his smile, then turn around only to find Fiona Greyson waiting, half hidden behind a large potted palm. I know when Charlie has the Churches behind closed doors because that's when she steps out, directly into my path.

"Do your husband and kids know you're having a little romance with my husband? Going to his house at all hours? Getting involved in dangerous crimes?" She stands tall, and although I'm just as tall as she is, I feel pretty small right now. She bats her eyes. "Of course, I would never say a thing. I'm not one to spread my hurts all over town. But…" She shrugs. "I'm not sure I can say the same for my friends. All my lifelong friends here, who know Charlie belongs with me, like I belong here on Sophia Island." Her eyes are cold with malice as she says, "Why don't you figure out where you belong… and go there."

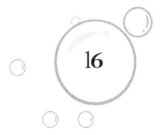

16

"Hey, Jewel, can you come in here?" I'm glad the door has closed behind the ice queen when I hear her husband's voice. I turn around and walk toward him. Charlie holds open the door to a small interrogation room, which we go in to sit across from each other at a table.

"Don't be intimidated by the room," he says. "It's just that it's quiet here. I'd thought we could talk at your house, but..." He shrugs at me.

I agree with a nod. He tries to continue, but I blurt out, "There was blood in the parking lot?"

"I cannot talk about that. Not one word. I need you to tell me everything you can think of about when Eden came home to change clothes Saturday night, but first"—he squints and tilts his head—"am I wrong, or did I hear someone gasp when the video was on? Especially when it looked like the man was going to turn his head to be seen?"

"I heard it, too, but I have no idea who it was. You think someone recognized him?"

"Could be. It's not Holloway, though. Although he was there around the same time."

"He told you that? He had to have seen who Eden was with. That's great." I'm excited until I pay attention to his face. "Wait, why isn't that great? I saw him Friday, and he has a thing for Eden. He would've been near her."

"We can't find him."

I find that, beyond blinking, I've forgotten how to move. "What do you mean you can't find him? Where does he live?"

"Jewel, I have people on it. Trust me, we'll find him. Right now I need to get your take on Eden from Saturday night. That's all, but it's important."

I close my eyes and take a deep breath. "I've tried to remember exactly what she said, and the closest I can get is that she said she was meeting some people or someone at The Sea Snake to listen to a band. I don't think she mentioned a guy, but something made me think a guy was involved. Maybe what she was wearing?" I shake my head, then focus on the wall behind him. "I questioned why she was changing if she'd been with these people all evening, and she said something about a friend, or a friend got a text? Or something." I look back at him. "What do her friends say?"

He heaves a sigh and leans back. "That they were downtown and no one wanted to go to The Sea Snake, but all of a sudden Eden wanted to go hear the band there. That a friend from Facebook was going to be there, and Eden wanted to go check him out. The friends she was with hadn't met him before and didn't know him."

"Hey!" I sit up fast. "Yeah, Facebook. It wasn't a text; it was a Facebook friend who was in town, and she wanted to surprise them. I don't think she said it was a guy, but the way she was acting and then what she came out of her room wearing, well, I was pretty sure it was a guy. So, is it the guy in the video? Did you find him on her Facebook?"

"Pretty sure it is." He leans forward, placing his forearms on the table. He lowers his head, then looks up at me. "It's a fake account. Aiden says the guy in the pictures looks somewhat like the guy that night, but not exactly. We've found the account the guy took the pictures from, but that guy lives out in Colorado, married with kids, in his mid-thirties. We can't find any way that he's related to Eden except he looks like our guy. And the pictures are old, mostly from his college years."

"So this guy made this Facebook page to attract women?" That description of something making your blood run cold? It's accurate. I shiver and hug myself. "That sounds like what human traffickers would do."

Charlie sucks his teeth for a moment, then pulls back. "I know, but I don't get that feeling with this. Looks like it was just about Eden, but experts are looking at it to see if this guy's profile has been used before." He leans forward and reaches out to cover my hands with his. "We're working on this, and we'll find her. We have things in the works, okay? Trust me."

"What things?" I ask, but he's already standing up.

"You with Annie? She's ready to go." He steps to the door and pulls it open. "Let me know if y'all think of anything. I'll keep you in the loop."

He ushers me out to the entryway where Annie is waiting. She waves at Charlie, but I can tell she wants him to leave. Once he does, she grabs my arm and propels us to the front doors. "I told them we came together so I had to wait for you. I've already texted the girls. We're meeting at Cherry's house."

"Annie, what's going on?"

Outside, the dull brightness of midday surprises me since it feels like I've been in the police station all day, but Annie keeps us moving until we get to her car. "They found Eden's car up in Kingsland, and Aiden is already headed there. He's not on duty, but they asked him to come look it over. He wants us to help him look around. We're going in Cherry's SUV."

"Kingsland? Where's that?"

"Just over the river in Georgia. Get in. Let's just leave your car here."

Remembering what my house was like and who was there when I left there this morning, I don't have to think long. I jump into the hot car. "Text Aiden and ask him if he knows the password to Eden's Facebook account."

Cherry is driving with Tamela beside her. Annie, Lucy, and I are in the back seat, and we've found Eden's stalker's Facebook page. We're ignoring the pictures since we know they're fake, but we've all agreed we would probably have gone to meet a guy who looked like that in a bar at midnight when we were in our twenties. I shudder, hoping my girls would've been more suspicious, but a good-looking guy you think is a friend is hard to pass up. Plus, Eden was on her home turf. Concentrating on just his Facebook conversations with Eden, this man comes off as a nice guy, but knowing now that he was fake, we can see how he's leading her on, how he's playing innocent and harmless. And, oh, he just happens to be on Sophia Island for just one night on his way south to make sure his grandmother is ready for the hurricane. How he never even remembered Eden lived on Sophia Island and how he'd love to see her in person for a few minutes, it makes my stomach hurt reading it now.

Lucy lets out a big huff. "But how did he find Eden? Why her? This all seems very specific."

Cherry speaks up from the driver's seat. "I have to agree. Just listening to you all while I'm driving, this doesn't sounds like some human trafficking scheme or serial killer."

"Why? What makes you say that?" I know I sound desperate, but Cherry is often the soul of common sense, a good quality in a nurse.

"Because they usually prey on vulnerable people. Those who need help and are alone. A large immigrant population is one of the reasons Florida is popular with these awful sorts. Also our tourism and travel industries. We're trained to look for warning signs at the hospital, and Eden doesn't match them." She pauses. "Of course, it's not foolproof."

I'm seated in the middle of Annie and Lucy. Annie lays her hand on mine and grasps it. "Cherry is right. That's what the police think too. At least that's what Charlie and Aiden think. Aiden just sent me a long text. The higher-ups are, well, they're ready to let some task force from Jacksonville have control and turn it into something bigger. Johnson's guys finished in record time with Eden's car and have moved on. They think it was a decoy or something."

Shifting my head, I see Tamela and Lucy making eye contact in the rearview mirror, and I can tell they aren't in such agreement that it's not something bigger, but wisely, compassionately, they say nothing. I calm down and turn to Annie. "Why do Aiden and Charlie think differently than the others? Does he say anything about, well, about the blood in the parking lot? Charlie said he couldn't talk about it. Not one word."

"Nothing on the blood. It's probably too early to know anything." She hems and haws a bit before blowing out a long breath. "Aiden's seen her car, and, well, he thinks she left him a note telling him she's okay and not to worry."

I squint at her. "A note? What else does it say? She wrote it and left it in the car? So maybe she did just run away?"

"No, it was kind of cryptic, and the police on the scene aren't sure that's what it is."

Tamela flops around in the front seat and demands, "Tell us what it is. Quit messing around!"

"Okay, okay." Annie picks up her phone and taps on it as she talks. "It's in lipstick, and it's on the inside of the passenger door, like she was writing while she was riding. Means someone else was driving. Here are the pictures."

Sure enough, there are bright, orange-red markings on the interior of a car door. Tamela has unbuckled her seat belt and is hanging over the middle to see the pictures with me and Lucy. When we finish and hand her phone back to her, the three of us are silent.

I meet Cherry's eyes in the rearview mirror and barely give her a shake of my head.

Annie looks at the pictures again. "I know you can't make heads nor tails of it, but Aiden says he can see clearly that she was writing 'OK' and 'Don't worry,' and I can kind of see those. But then the mess he believes says something like 'Prank'? Well, that I'm just not seeing."

"Prank?" Lucy says. "Give me that phone back. Where does he see it say 'prank'?"

We study the scribbles but never come up with "prank," or the other words either. As Cherry pulls up to a stoplight on the highway, she says, "But Aiden knows these marks were made just this weekend?"

Annie nods enthusiastically, then seems to think it over before shrugging. "Well, he's pretty sure."

We all groan as the light changes and Cherry turns left into a shopping center. "This is where we're meeting him right?"

Annie confirms, "Yep. He's getting a sandwich here."

We spot him at a round, concrete picnic table outside the restaurant. There's just a dot of shade on the table, but he's got most of himself in it. We pile out and find seats around him also scrunching forward to share the shade. We wait for him to finish his last bite as patiently as we can. He's not exactly looking at us, but then he sucks in a breath and glares at his mother. "You just couldn't help it. Had to get in a fight with Eden's mother with all those television cameras right there. Even Belle's station is showing it. She says she can't help it. It's news!"

"Son, Kerry thinks you had something to do with all this."

He interrupts her. "And now the whole world thinks it too. I'm just lucky I'm not in some jail cell right now!"

Annie's eyes are wide and her mouth shut. Lucy is on Aiden's other side, and she puts a hand on his shoulder. "Aiden. Aiden, look at me." He reluctantly does. "Now take a slow breath. Everyone understands that emotions are running high. The TV people just have nothing better to show right now." He opens his mouth and starts to turn around to yell at his mother again, but Lucy pinches his shoulder. The way he jerks and his eyebrows jump, it's obvious Lucy knows what she's doing. She again has his full attention.

"The best way to get all that off folks' screens is to find Eden. Taking all your frustrations out on your mom isn't going to help." Then she tips her head to give her look a little more menace. "Believe me, your mother has some bones to pick with you, too, don't you figure?" He thinks on that for moment, and then he meekly nods. She smiles, releases her grasp on him, and pats him on the back.

Aiden looks at Annie, gives her a small smile, and clears his throat. "Okay, here's what I know and why I need y'all's help. She's here. I can feel it. Her car is fine. It's not parked erratically or unlawfully. If I didn't know her better, I'd swear she just took a couple days to get away, except…"

"Except for the Facebook guy, right?" I ask.

He nods. "Exactly. It's some kind of a set-up, but she wasn't afraid. Believe me, if Eden had been afraid, she would've done more than leave me some lipstick notes. Y'all know her. She wouldn't go quietly."

Lucy leans forward. "So about these notes. These are new in her car?"

"Absolutely," he assures us. "Well, I think they are. I mean, what else could they be?" Tamela groans as he rushes on. "But listen! She left The Sea Snake with this guy. I know he was fooling her online, but he didn't force her to go with him. I was watching them at the bar. I could tell she liked him." He scoffs. "She couldn't like a killer."

Now there are more groans, and my worry gets a boost. He ignores us and stands up. "I'm going in to get a drink refill, and then we have to get to work. I appreciate y'all's help." He's a couple of steps away when he turns back to us. "And, uh, could y'all not say anything about being up here with me? I'm kind of in trouble, and I'm not supposed to be, you know, here." He shakes his head and continues on.

Once he's out of earshot, Annie says, "Guys, we have to help him. What else are we going to do? He's very certain that she's in this area."

The rest of us look at each other and come to an agreement without saying a word. I answer for us all. "Of course we'll help. Whatever we can do to find her."

Aiden comes out and picks up the notebook he'd been writing in. "Okay. Y'all are going to split up into pairs, and we're going to talk to people and just look for anything suspicious."

Annie is the only one who really believes in Aiden's plan at this point, but the rest of us are smiling and nodding and going along with it. I think the police are letting the young officer run with this idea to keep him out of their way. That thought makes me incredibly sad, even as I realize it's not a bad plan on their part. We can help by keeping Annie out of their way too.

It's good to have something to do other than sit around my house waiting for bad news with the group that was there this morning. Besides, I saw The Annie and Kerry Show in real life; I don't need any replays on TV.

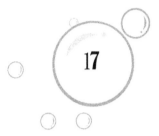

17

Annie climbs in the front seat of Aiden's beige Toyota, and I climb in the back. She rolls her eyes at me but talks to him. "If you'd mentioned splitting up in your text, we'd have driven more than one car."

"Whatever, Momma. Let's just go. Sorry about the mess in the back seat, Miss Jewel."

"No worries. I remember my kids' cars." I collect empty fast food wrappers and water bottles into a plastic grocery store bag. When it's full, I set it in the floorboard on the other side of the car, then throw the rest of the garbage around it. "So, where was Eden's car found? Kingsland, I think your mom said?"

"Not exactly. Kingsland is the bigger town at the interstate, and then out this way is the sub base." He meets my eyes. "You know, Kings Bay Submarine Base?"

"Oh, I have heard of that. That's where the submarines people talk about in the river come from, right?"

"Yes, ma'am. It's a pretty big operation. Matter of fact, lots of folks in Sophia Beach first came to the area when they were stationed at Kings Bay. Anyway, St. Mary's is actually the town it's in, and Eden's car was found there. That's where we're headed."

Annie looks back at me. "It's a really cute historic area with some of the best seafood at Lane's, right on the water. It's more like the old-fashioned seafood places from when we were growing up."

As the street narrows, the trees get bigger and hang out over the asphalt ahead, draping their moss almost to the sidewalk. The houses grow more historic, and ahead I can see the waterfront, but then Aiden takes a left and we're driving through a neighborhood. With a couple more turns, we're at the entrance to a sprawling cemetery. He stops the car, and we're left listening to the air conditioner while he looks around. "There he is," he says as a small truck pulls up beside us. "Wait here and I'll go talk to Johnny." He gets out of the car and into the passenger side of the truck.

Annie waves at the driver of the truck.

"Do you know him?" I ask.

"Yeah, some. He's from Sophia but works up here. He and Aiden have been friends for a long time." She turns to look at me, and her eyebrows are raised. "Friends against my advice. Johnny's a troublemaker, but I guess in this kind of a situation that's probably who you need to talk to."

She points out the windshield. "See, over there is the river, and from there you can see Sophia Island. This is where you get the ferry to go to Cumberland Island. We were on the ferry one time, and it had to stop to let a submarine go by. We just could just see the top; crazy to think a whole submarine was under the water right there. They do a lot of work to make sure the channel is deep enough. They dredge up the bottom pretty often."

Aiden jogs toward us and gets back in the driver's seat. His friend's truck peels out of the sandy lot. "Johnny's been asking around for me, and he says a guy like the one I described has been seen around town, mostly picking up food and stuff. Even in a military town, or maybe especially in a military town, people pay attention to strangers."

"So you really think she might still be in the area?" I feel hopeful for the first time all day.

"I do." He takes in a deep breath, then releases it. "We've got some more good news. One of my buddies let me know they've got a lead on Holloway. Some video from The Sea Snake someone took that he's in. Never thought I'd say it, but his watching Eden might turn out to be a good thing. Hopefully he saw something."

Annie scowls at him. "That's that guy from the coffee shop Jewel was talking about, right? I never did like the way he looked at her, but she said he was harmless. What's he got to do with all this?"

Aiden explains, "He was at The Sea Snake Saturday night. I didn't know he hung out there. Doesn't seem like his scene. He's more the slimy type to hang out at the hotel bars, I've always thought, but there he was grinning on the sidelines while I was fighting with Eden." He heaves a deep sigh and shakes his head. "I'm such an idiot. I've got to find her so I can tell her she's right. I do need to grow up. Even if she hates me, she's got to know she was right."

He turns the car around in the sand and heads down a small side road. Through the trees of the cemetery, I can see the water and the park alongside it. The silence in the car is thick, so I say in a light voice, "This really does look like a charming little town."

Annie jumps in to agree. "I always forget about it. We'll definitely come up here one day to walk around and have lunch at Lane's. The park along the water even has wooden porch swings to sit in and look out at the river."

At the main street, with the big trees full of moss, we turn to the left and drive away from the water. Once we get away from the historic area and its low speed limit, Aiden roars up the highway. After a couple of minutes, he steers into a gravel parking lot beside a small place with an old, faded banner draped across the front dubbing it Jeepers Bar & Grill. He jerks open his door but says, "Y'all stay here. I'll be right back."

Annie sits still, watching her son, but as soon as he's inside, she's all action. "Let's go." I kind of thought that was going to happen, so I already had my seat belt off. I can't help but smile as I follow her across the gravel and to the door. We open it and step into the darkness. At the first sniff, my stomach growls. Annie nods. "I agree. Something smells delicious."

"Ladies," the man behind the bar says, which causes the young man he's talking to to turn around. A young man named Aiden Bryant.

He grunts, "Didn't I say for y'all to stay in the car?"

Annie keeps walking toward him. "We're hungry and we have to go the bathroom. Right, Jewel?"

My stomach growls again in response, and the man Aiden's talking to laughs. "The ladies are hungry. Whatcha gonna do?" He turns to the small window behind him and, I assume, places our order for us because he tells us it'll be out shortly. Aiden shakes his head but points us to a table. I go to sit down, but Annie heads to the restroom.

The small, dark barroom is clean, but customers are sparse. Makes sense: it is a beautiful summer afternoon to be hanging out indoors. Before Aiden finishes talking to the man behind the counter, another man comes from the kitchen carrying two plates. He sits them down at my table, then points to the cooler beside the bar. "Get ya a drink there or order from Barnie," he says as he walks away.

Aiden goes to the cooler and looks at me. "A water is good," I say, and he pulls two out before coming to the table, arriving just before his mother.

"Well, that was fast," she says. "Barbecue? Oh, and fried okra and slaw. I bet it's delicious."

I've already learned that barbecue down here means meat with some kind of sauce on it, not grilling out. I've also learned it's pretty much all delicious. I have not sworn an oath to a particular type of sauce as apparently one is supposed to. I think it's all good, and this is no exception.

Pointing my fork at Aiden, I tell him to help himself to my okra. "I don't think I'd like it."

Annie rolls her eyes. "We'll talk about that another time. So, what did he say?"

"He's seen our guy. I've already called Greyson, and he's sending some guys here. He says the focus is still in the Jacksonville direction because, well, they found her purse down there."

Annie and I straighten up. "Where? Is her phone in it?" I ask.

"No, but they got some pings for it. Again in that direction." He frowns as he thinks. "That doesn't make sense. How did her car get up here and her stuff down there? That's almost an hour apart on the interstate, and Sophia Beach is miles off the interstate."

Annie pats her son's hand. "The important thing is that we're making progress. Progress in two areas is better than no progress in, well, zero areas." She frowns, then smiles at him.

He gives her a small smile back. "Anyway, I also called Mrs. Berry and the other ladies, and they're going to come pick y'all up. I didn't want you around if things got dicey, but now I don't know what to think. But whatever, y'all need to go on home." He stands up and pushes his chair back under the table. "Now, Momma, don't get mad. I wasn't sure this would pan out, and I never thought we'd get a lead this fast. So…" But he stops talking and just stands there because his mother isn't even looking at him. She's eating calmly and ignoring him.

Between bites she says, "Go on. Do what you need to. I have things to do also."

He and I look at each other, and then he leans on the back of the chair. "Like what, Momma?"

She shrugs and takes a sip from her water bottle. "Like I have some ideas where she might be."

"Really?" I can't help but blurt out.

She frowns at me. "Really."

Aiden pulls his chair back out and perches on the edge of it. "Okay. Where?"

She doesn't even pretend not to preen. "We passed a sign for a campground back there. If this guy doesn't live around here, wouldn't that be a good place to hide out?"

"It would. But, Momma, you can't be messing around now. We're talking about Eden's life, and the police are on their way. What if this guy's not dangerous to Eden because he doesn't think he'll get caught?"

"He's right, Annie. We need to stay out of their way." I turn to Aiden. "But she's right too. That is a good idea about the campground. You're going to tell Charlie?"

"Right this minute." He shows us his phone, which is dialing Charlie's number as he stands. "Now I'm going to meet the guys. Y'all enjoy your lunch. Your friends will be here in a minute. Thanks for your help. Really…" He pauses and swallows. "I appreciate y'all having my back when no one else did." He clears his throat and leaves quickly.

We watch him, and then we both sigh. I nod and sigh again, more deeply this time. "I feel good about this. Doesn't sound like this guy wants to hurt her or take her off somewhere. You know?"

Annie smiles in agreement; then she looks at my plate and gives me a cocked eyebrow. "Okay, about that okra…"

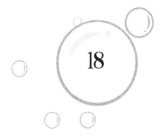

18

As we were walking into my house, I warned
Annie to keep a low profile. She said she just
wanted to be here when we learn that Eden
is safe and sound. I really couldn't make her
stay away since the other ladies from our
lunch bunch were coming over. I've never
understood the need for what the kids call
"a posse," but no way did I want to spend
any more time on my own with Galena and
her friends. Cathy's fine and Galena's okay,
but when you throw Fiona into the mix…
Anyway, Annie had been instructed to keep
a low profile.

Stupid me.

"Well, Aiden cracked the case. Eden
should be safe and sound any minute!" Annie announces.

That brings people from all over: Galena and two ladies from the kitchen, Cathy from upstairs, and Fiona, well, she did look up from her magazine where she's comfortably stretched out in the living room.

On my chaise lounge.

Galena is clapping her hands. "You did it! You found her!"

"Not exactly," I try to say, but Cathy cuts me off, waving her hands.

She cuts all of us off as she hurries toward us. "Be quiet. I finally got Kerry to sleep."

I step in her direction. "That's good, but she'd probably want to know."

Cathy furrows her forehead. "What? That maybe there's some hope? Then to only have to deal with that hope fading out to nothing?"

I'm taken aback by Cathy's pessimism. While a little off, she's been fairly optimistic up till now, I think. I mean there was all the spirit talk, but otherwise.

"But it is hopeful," Lucy says. With her chin tilted up, she walks past Cathy toward the stairs. Cathy may be used to being listened to and heeded, but so is Lucy, and she's not going to be deterred. "I haven't seen Kerry in all this, so I'll go talk to her."

Cathy shrugs behind Lucy's back and

turns purposefully toward me. "So you've found her. Where is she? I assume she's in good health? When will she be arriving here? Shouldn't you call Ted and tell him the good news?"

Over her head, I watch Lucy's advance up the stairs slow until she stops. She turns around and quietly comes back down. "Well, I guess we don't really know a lot, do we?"

Cathy's face fills with disappointment as she looks at us. She then floats past me into the kitchen, saying, "I could use a cup of coffee."

Fiona stretches out like a cat waking from a nap in my chair. "This is such a nice piece of furniture. So comfortable. Did it come with the rest of your, uh, décor, Jewel?" She scoots to the edge and then stands. "I guess Charlie is letting you ladies take credit for another crime solved? I'm not sure why the city even keeps paying him with you Nosy Nellies on the case. So, tell us how you solved this one." The look she gives us is the opposite of interested.

Annie blusters, "Aiden solved it. He and Eden have a connection. A real connection. We should hear from him soon." She says this firmly, but as she looks at me, then at her other friends, her eyes lose their confidence. "I hope."

"Whatever," Fiona mutters as she avoids walking near any of us, goes down the back hall, and enters the rear kitchen door.

Galena grabs Annie's arm. "I'm sure it will all turn out fine. Now, you ladies come have something to eat. There's quite a selection. People have been bringing food all morning."

Annie goes with her, telling her she's just had lunch. Tamela, Cherry, and Lucy all come toward me, Tamela squinting. "Are you sure it's okay if we're here? We don't want to leave you, but…"

Lucy finishes for her. "But it feels kind of crowded. I am hungry, though." She looks at her watch. "Plus, I'd hate to leave before we hear something."

"Have something to eat." I say. "I'm going upstairs to change, and I'll look in on Kerry. Wonder where Ted is."

We split up, with them headed toward the food and me going upstairs.

While the rest of my friends were in casual and comfortable clothes, I'd fallen into the funeral clothes trap. I admonish myself as I undress at how I'm letting Fiona get under my skin. I didn't exactly dress up as much as her group did to go to the police station, but I did put on low heels and a sleeveless dark dress. I change out of that and pull on a pair of white capris, a long, bright-blue shirt, and white gym shoes. Or tennis shoes, as my friends here call them.

As I sit on my bed, my optimism from earlier leaks away. I'd known it was silly to get my hopes up. It's probably good Kerry is asleep. I have a feeling the minutes are going to feel like hours this afternoon. Who knows when we'll hear anything?

I get up from the bed with a groan and walk quietly down the hall. Hearing a soft noise from Eden's room, I ease open the door to peek in.

Kerry waves at me, then croaks, "Come in." Her face creases as I get closer. "Did you find her?"

"We got a really good lead, and Aiden feels like she's all right."

She closes her eyes. "Please don't say his name. This is all his fault."

I sit on the edge of the bed at her knees. "But he might be the reason we find her."

Kerry's eyes open, and tears spill out. "No. We won't find her now. It's been too long."

"Don't say that. You can't give up hope. I

really feel very hopeful after being with, uh, the police."

She shuffles around in the bed, and I get up as she maneuvers to sit on the edge of the mattress. She swipes at tears as they run down her face, then reaches into the pocket of the black dress she's had on all day. "Because you didn't see these."

She dumps a handful of notes onto the bed. They are torn pieces of paper with writing on them. I straighten a couple out.

She's gone. No hope now. Cry your eyes out. Then I gasp as I see another one: *She's better off.*

I sit back down on the other side of her. "Kerry, what are these?"

"We've been getting them off and on this past week, but we were just ignoring them. Trashing them without reading them at first. Then Ted remembered them this morning, and it makes sense. It's like God is talking to us through these notes."

"These are not from God. Does Charlie know about them?"

"Why? He doesn't care. We're cursed, and now we've lost Eden."

The door pushes open, and after a moment's hesitation, Cathy comes in. "Oh, she's awake." She squints at the bed, then reaches for one of the notes. "Sweetie, what are these?"

"Those notes I told you about. Ted brought them to me when he came a bit ago. I was just telling Jewel we'd forgotten about them, but then when he went home last night, there were more of them under the doors and even in the shop."

Cathy grows more alarmed as she reads them. "In the shop? Did he see anyone leave them? I had no idea they were like this."

Kerry shakes her head, and more tendrils fall from her heavy braid. "No, he doesn't know how long they'd been there. We rarely use the back door, and there were a couple there. And the one in the shop was under some other stuff. He's not very organized. Besides, I don't think a person left them."

Cathy kneels at our feet, her hands on Kerry's knees. "You said you thought you knew who they were from?"

"Well, you know. Ted sometimes makes people mad." She still stares straight ahead.

I get her attention, which is difficult as she's definitely not completely here with us. "Where is Ted?"

"I don't know. Maybe downstairs?"

Cathy whispers to me. "Why don't you go find him and I'll stay here with her?"

I don't like the idea of Kerry staying up here in this darkened bedroom. It's like she's already in mourning. "Kerry, come downstairs. Have something to eat? Or, I know, a cup of tea?"

She shrugs but doesn't look at me. Cathy sits beside her and hugs her shoulders. "That does sound good. We'll be right down."

At the door, I look back and see Cathy collecting the notes and laying them on the night table as she talks softly to Kerry. Poor Kerry. This might've driven her right around the bend. We have to get some good news fast. Did she mean God when she told Cathy she might know who they were from? I need to talk to Charlie.

At the bottom of the stairs, I turn to the left and then close myself in Craig's old office. Aiden answers on the first ring, and I ask, "Any news?"

"We're looking. The campground was a good idea, but we've found nothing. How are things there?"

"Okay. Um, is Charlie there?" Talking to him on Aiden's phone is not the same as calling him, right?

"No. I'm still on my own. This jerk with the task force from Jacksonville says I'm a person of interest, so I can't be involved in the official search, but the guys are keeping me in the loop."

"Aiden, person of interest sounds serious. Maybe you should back off, let the others find Eden. You don't want people blaming you for anything."

"Don't go telling my mom, all right? This is all my fault. If we hadn't been fighting, Eden wouldn't have been at The Sea Snake drinking like that. I deserve to be blamed. I've gotta go."

He hangs up, and I do what I swore I wasn't going to do. At least not with his wife in the next room.

"Jewel. Are you okay?" Charlie answers.

His low voice, so concerned, catches me off guard. "I'm fine." I shake my head to clear it and remember everything I want to ask him. "Do you know Ted and Kerry are getting these really creepy notes like, 'She's better off,' and that they shouldn't have any hope?"

"No. When?"

"Kerry was really vague. I think she's taken something. I'm going to find Ted and see what he knows. But the notes have been left all around their shop and apartment, and they are really scary. They seem to pertain to Eden going missing. Maybe that guy has been back in the area during all this. But then Kerry also said Ted has made a lot of people mad. What's that about?"

"It's about Ted Church. He's always considered himself a pseudo-hippie. He was too young in the sixties; plus, I don't think he ever had the gumption to actually rebel against anything. Half the crazy letters to the editor in the paper are by him, but he changes his name. Old regulars like me know the names he uses." He pauses as if to control his rising temper. "Ted is a real piece of work that has rubbed a lot of people the wrong way. I actually have done some digging in that direction to see if he's angered someone enough for them to take Eden. Someone from here wouldn't have a hard time getting close enough to her. I did it off the books, of course. It's a long shot, but these notes sound just like some of the kooks in town he's argued with over the years. I'm probably just grasping at straws. Anyway, I'll have an officer come collect the notes. Anything else?"

"Yeah, have you found Holloway?"

The phone goes quiet. Then he clears his throat. "He's dead."

My throat tightens, and I gulp for air. "How? Where?"

"Listen, it's not good. When we looked

him up, the computer lit up like Christmas. He's been in and out of jail and owes some not very good people a lot of money."

"So they killed him? Nothing to do with Eden?"

"Not sure. We didn't get to him quick enough. There was some blood found in the parking lot at The Sea Snake. That in and of itself isn't alarming; it's a rough bar. But with Eden's disappearance, we tested it. When we got into Holloway's house, we found him dead from a day-old head wound, and the blood in the parking lot could be a match for him. Looks like he was in some kind of a scuffle, fell, and hit his head on a chunk of concrete. Laid there for a while, then managed to get up and drive home. Went to bed and died in his sleep. We don't know who's responsible or what he was into that night. We're looking into it. Like everything else."

"Maybe he saw who took Eden and tried to stop it"—I catch a sob in my throat—"and died for it. Oh my God. The person who has Eden left a man to bleed to death in a dark parking lot."

"We don't know that. Don't tell anyone there, okay?"

I sniff a couple of times and wipe my nose on my palm. "Okay. But what about these bad guys you say he owed money?" I stop myself and take a breath. "I know. You're looking into it. So, what should I do?"

"Well, you called me looking for Ted, and I have a feeling I know where he's is."

"Where?"

All I hear is Charlie breathing, and then he clears his throat. "At his girlfriend's house. I'll send you the address."

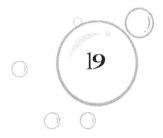

19

A tall, square-shouldered Black woman, my age or older, answers the doorbell. "Can I help you?"

"I'm looking for Ted Church?"

She smiles. "You're Miss Mantelle."

As she's saying that, I cock my head. "We've met, haven't we?"

"Yes, ma'am. I'm the administrator at the police station. Naomi Jones."

"That's right. Call me Jewel."

"And you can call me Naomi." Then she steps inside and motions for me to follow her. I can't help but wonder if Kerry knows about this woman and her husband? But I firmly stop myself, I have enough to think about without adding Ted Church's complicated life to the mix.

"Ted, hon, you've got company," she says loudly as we walk across the hardwood floors through the living room, then the kitchen, onto a small sun porch. There we find Ted at a table with lots of papers in front of him, along with his phone and a china cup of green tea.

He jumps up from his seat. "Jewel. Any word? I've been tearing my hair out trying to figure out who took my girl, but nothing. Nothing at all!" He pulls on his gray ponytail and plops back down in his chair.

Naomi draws in a breath through her nose, then asks sweetly, "Can I get you some tea or water? We're having some calming tea before I have to go back to work."

I tear my eyes off Eden's father to look at our host. "No, I'm fine. I won't bother you long."

I sit down in the wicker chair next to him as she goes back into the kitchen. "Ted, those notes you brought to Kerry. What's up with those?"

He looks up at me, his readers hanging low on his nose. "I don't know. Are they from that kidnapper? Or some disgruntled customer or someone who's always disliked me or hates tattoos? I've not ever really worried about making people happy. I'm going through my records looking now, but I think it's a love triangle involving that Aiden, Eden, and this mystery man no one can find. I don't think it has anything to do with me and Kerry and the shop at all."

Naomi carries her tea into the sun porch and sits on a wicker couch. "He's doesn't know what he's talking about, of course. I've told him when I get back to the station I'm telling everyone about those notes. Maybe they're from one of the knuckleheads around here, I've not seen them, but they are definitely clues." She studies me. "Have you seen them?"

"Yes. And they are very creepy. Um." I hesitate when it comes to saying Kerry's name, but Naomi does it for me.

"Let me guess: Kerry thinks they're from some ghost or something?"

I smile in relief. "Yeah, something like that. Listen, Ted, have you seen anyone that looks kind of like this around the shop?" I hold up a picture of the Facebook guy that Aiden says looks the most like the guy from The Sea Snake.

He studies it. He even takes my phone, adjusts his glasses, and really looks at it. "Maybe a little older than this? He looks a little heavier. They showed us this guy earlier, but I wasn't thinking about the shop. I was thinking of if he was a friend of Eden's."

"Yeah, so you have seen him?"

He goes back to studying his papers. "I think so. Maybe. He's just been around. Maybe in the shop a time or two but didn't want to talk."

Naomi pulls out her phone. "I'm calling Charlie now. I've had enough of you trying to leave the police out of this. That sweet Eden shouldn't have to pay for your hardheadedness about the cops." She listens to ringing as she mutters, "I mean, I'm practically police, and you've never had no problem with me."

Ted stares at her for a moment, lets out a huff, and then begins collecting his papers. "I knew coming here was a mistake! You don't understand a thing. You'll be lucky if you ever see me again!" he shouts as he stomps past us and through the house. We hear the front door slam.

Charlie has answered, but Naomi stops talking to him to say to me, "Hope you didn't block him in."

I shake my head no and start to stand, but she lays a hand on my arm. "Stay a minute."

She talks to Charlie and winks at me when she tells him I'm sitting there. She hangs up and then sits back to sip her tea.

"Don't worry about Ted. He's just angry that he can't do anything to help Eden. He doesn't like the police, and depending on them is not something he's ever going to do easily."

"But like you said, you're practically police."

She grins. "Child. I could be head of the FBI in Washington, DC, and Ted Church would find his way to my door. We've been friends since before he even knew what he thought."

"So, what does Charlie think?" I don't mention that I'd told Charlie about the notes, since it doesn't sound like he mentioned it.

"He's sending Officer Weber over to pick up the notes. He agrees that they sound important. Maybe you should get to your house before the officer shows up." She gets up from the couch with the floral cushion. "I've got to get back to work anyway."

"Good idea." I follow her back through her house and find that I love how tiny and perfect it is. It's so comfortable. "I love your house."

"It was my mother's. She passed on a few years ago, and slowly I've made it more mine than hers."

"So you grew up here?"

"I sure did. I've lived here my entire life."

"Ted's from here, too, right?"

"Yes, ma'am. Right over there?" She points out her front door. "That house was where his folks lived. They're both gone now." As I walk out onto the front stoop, she says she's glad I stopped by.

"I am too. I hate that it's under such awful circumstances, but, you know, if you ever want to stop in and see my house, you know, the Mantelle Mansion," I say with a laugh, "like so many folks from around here seem to want to do, please feel free. I know it was off limits to folks for years. We could have coffee or even lunch."

She laughs. "Oh, honey. I've been in that house dozens of times. That Corabelle had problems with her hoity-toity neighbors, but she enjoyed having regular folks over. I'm the one that drove her to the old folks home when she left."

My mouth is hanging open, and she winks again and chuckles. "Thank you. I'd love to stop and have coffee with you one morning, but we'll talk later, Jewel. Right now we need to help these clueless men find that girl."

"What do you mean they're gone?" I ask

young Officer Weber, a petite, dark-haired young woman.

She jerks her head at Kerry, who was standing beside the front door talking to her when I got home. "That's what she just said. Officer Greyson says you saw the notes?"

Fiona laughs. "Of course she's the one that told Charlie."

Kerry turns on me. "I didn't give you permission to tell the police!"

"We're trying to find your daughter. Of course I told the police." I push past her and head to the stairs. "Officer Weber, come up here. I'll show you."

I rush up the stairs and find Lucy and Annie in Eden's room. "What are you two doing here?"

They startle, then hold out a metal wastebasket toward me. Annie explains, "We smelled smoke, ran up here, and found this burning."

The officer steps into the room and reaches for the basket. She looks inside. "Nothing but ash."

I've moved past my friends and am pulling back the bed covers, looking for any of the notes Kerry might've missed. "Why would she burn them?"

Cathy speaks from the door. "Kerry says

she didn't want to share them. It's sad, but she really feels it's too late to find her daughter." She throws her hands up. "I went to the restroom while she was freshening up. Then she was in the hall waiting for me when I came out of the restroom, and we went downstairs to get some tea. I was in the kitchen and didn't even smell the smoke."

Officer Weber hands me her phone. "Here. Officer Greyson wants to talk to you."

I ignore the phone and walk around her. "Not unless he's calling to say he found Eden." At the bedroom door, I look back in. "Did he?"

She pulls the phone to her face. "She wants to know if you found Miss Church." She shakes her head at me and then holds the phone out again. I ignore her again and walk down the hall to my bedroom. There I slam the door and lie face down on my bed. My head hurts, and I'm so very tired. I'm starting to hate my own house because of all those awful women downstairs, hanging out like food-pushing ghouls. I roll over and take some deep breaths. My phone buzzes in my pocket and I pull it out, but I don't look at it. In the bathroom I down a couple of ibuprofen and a big glass of water. I wash my face and finally go back to sit on the bed and look at my phone.

The text is from Charlie. "Tommy Tompkins at Shark Hunt—can you and Annie talk to him? She knows him. He's out on North Beach."

"Why not," I answer out loud and also in a return text. Then I forward Charlie's text to Annie and add, "Meet me on the front porch in five."

I don't wait for her response. This is a good thing I've recently discovered about having friends: You know what they're going to say before you even ask the question.

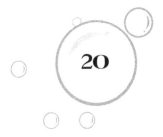

20

"Gonna pull in here and fill up," Annie says as we ease into a gas station. She's fumbling around with her purse, getting her credit card out of her wallet, all the while talking about it being "good just in case" and saying, "It never goes bad," and, "You know it'll get crazier later if things progress." She flings open her door, and as she's getting out, I still haven't put together what in the world she's talking about.

"What in the world are you talking about?" I ask before she closes the door.

"The hurricane. Just in case."

My heart freezes. I completely forgot about the hurricane. What did they name it? Oh no, how did I forget about it? I jerk my phone out of my purse, find my weather app, and look up the radar. I let out a deep breath. It's just where I left it, still off the coast somewhere down south. My heart thumps back to life, and I swallow the fear that had jumped into my mouth.

When Annie climbs back in the car, I laugh. "You really got me. Scared me to death in fact. The hurricane is still where it was this weekend."

She concentrates as she pulls out of the station, and then we're back on A1A for only a minute before she pulls into the main entrance of the state park. The park centers on an old brick fort at the mouth of the river. I explored it one afternoon this summer with Chris, though we went in the afternoon, when it was too hot to stay long. From the top you look out onto the ocean and river. Below there are lots of small rooms and passageways inside the walls.

Annie pays the fee to get into the park, and we're leisurely heading down the shady road. Huge trees form a moss-and-leaf tunnel, and it's like the noise and temperature of an August afternoon just faded away. Then I realize the noise I'm missing is Annie.

"So, what are you thinking?" I ask as I study her profile. She's frowning with her mouth twisted up tight.

"Trying to talk myself out of being honest with you."

"About Eden? Why? What are you thinking?"

"No, hon. No, about the hurricane."

"What about the hurricane?" My voice falls an octave as my breathing picks up its pace.

"See, there's several things you keep an eye on. You're right. It's still where it was this weekend, but it's gotten stronger." She winces as she takes a look at me. "It's up to a Category 3, and the water's so warm they think it could even get up to a 4."

"But, a four, is that really bad? I mean, I think that's really bad, right?"

"It can be. But it definitely means we have to keep an eye on it. Not panic, just keep an eye on it. And do things like fill up with gas and have water on hand. Honestly, for us here, it's more about being ready to deal with a long power outage than anything."

"But why do you need gas?"

She shrugs, and I can tell she's trying to keep me from panicking. "In case we have to evacuate the island; you don't want to be looking for gas then. But we rarely have ever had to evacuate."

"Evacuate? Are we still in that cone? Is the

cone bigger now that it's a four?" I'm staring at my phone, but I've lost all service this deep into the park, so I can't check for myself.

"Oh, well," she says with a shrug as we turn off the main park road to the right, and immediately we come out from under the low branches. The bushes around us grow thin and straggly, and I can feel we're heading toward the beach. I know what her shrug this time meant: We are most definitely in the cone. Probably right smack dab in the center, but well, there's nothing I can do about that now, when I don't have cell service.

I keep refreshing my phone anyway. We're going to talk to this man, find Eden, and then? I don't know—whatever they tell me to do, right after I have a good old-fashioned panic attack.

Annie says, "There's Tommy's truck. Did Charlie say anything more about what he wants to know?"

"Just that the kidnapper guy apparently was down here looking for sharks' teeth. Says he had an officer talk to Tommy already, but he feels he'd talk more freely to us. You know him?"

She pulls on a visor and opens her car door. "Oh yeah. He's always been around, but he's kind of grouchy. He's hunted for sharks' teeth since I've known him. Now he's turned it into a nice little business from what I hear. Well, I guess it's really his daughter that's made it a business." We've walked to the edge of the parking lot, and she's scanning the beach stretched out in front of us. I can see where the pier used to be, off to our left. I'd heard it went way out where the river and ocean meet but was damaged beyond repair in a hurricane a few years ago. Whoa. Just that thought makes my heart skip a beat and my mouth dry out. I forcefully turn away from that view just as Annie points.

"There he is. Tommy! Hey, Tommy!" she yells while we begin walking across the hot sand. I have on flip-flops, and the sand I feel around the edges is blazing hot. I hurry to get to where the sand is more packed down and stop there to look at the wide beach and big waves. That sure is a lot of water out there, and I sure do live on a small island. I look south, down the beach, but I can't imagine a hurricane just sitting out there. I feel like I'm being stalked. I swallow and hurry over to Annie. I reach her just as she reaches the shark guy.

"Hey, Tommy, this is my friend Jewel. Charlie Greyson told us we might should talk to you."

He's somewhere in his fifties, maybe sixties, I'd guess, but his dark, leathered skin is hard to read. His hair is cut short, so I can't tell if it's blond or gray.

He squints up at me, then straightens his ball cap as he saws his jaw back and forth before he talks. "Yeah. That guy. One cops think mighta went off with Eden? Pretty sure I talked to him a couple times last week."

Annie looks around. "Here? On the beach?"

"Yep. He tried to glom on to one of my groups. Ya know, folks pay good money to take one of my shark tooth tours, but you'd be amazed how many people try to hang around on the edges and hear what I'm saying. There's just some cheap sons of guns out there. Why, one guy—"

"Tommy, we don't have time for that right now. We need to find Eden, right?"

He rears back and stares at her, scoffing in disgust. "I know that. I'm the one who called the police in the first place. I'm the one who's actually trying to help here. You want to hear what I know or what?"

Annie gives me a look just short of rolling her eyes, then smiles and reaches out to lay a hand on Tommy's bare arm. "You're right, Tommy. Please understand I'm just worried about Eden." She sniffles. "I'm sorry. So I take it this guy wasn't on your tour, but he was trying to listen in."

After a nod of understanding, he pauses for effect, and I can see why his tours are so popular. He's a storyteller. "Yes, ma'am, the first time. So I just gave him the evil eye and moved away from him. Second time, though, I was down here by myself, and he came up and apologized."

"Apologized?" I ask, shaking my head. "That doesn't sound like a kidnapper."

"He didn't act like no kidnapper. Real interested in sharks. He'd managed to find only one shark's tooth, so I gave him some tips. Like getting a sieve, looking along the shell lines. See there, the ribbon in the sand with that kinda red tint? That's where I find a lot."

I find myself looking at our feet. "You said get a sieve? One on the end of a stick like those people have?" I point toward the water where an older couple are walking, staring at the sand as they scoop and search.

"That works, or even one like you have in your kitchen, a bowl. Once you get good at seeing them, you don't really need one. When they dredge the channel for the subs, it stirs up all the old sediment, and we get a fresh supply with every tide." He pulls his hand out of his pocket and opens it to reveal three small, black sharks' teeth.

"Subs? You mean the submarines? So all these being here doesn't just mean that there's a lot of sharks in this area?"

He chuckles. "No, ma'am. These are actually fossils. The sharks that lost these teeth lived thousands and thousands of years ago."

Annie blows out a breath and fans herself. "Okay, you two, we're not here for a lesson. It's too hot for that. Did this guy say anything to do with Eden?"

"Not per se. As much as I don't cotton to tattling to the police every little thing, I'da come clean if I had real information to help the girl. You know that, Annie. Charlie knows that."

"Of course. So, what did he have to say?" Annie asks, and we can hear her patience running out.

"He was just real interested in sharks and all that I was talking about. He said something about having been here before and losing something, or leaving something here."

That gets me to look up from my feet. "Losing something on the beach? Do you think that's what he was hunting for?"

"No." Tommy turns to look down the beach, like he's recalling the conversation.

"No, it was more like he lost a friend. Maybe he had a fight with someone? No, he seemed more sad than mad. He did say that sharks were a connection with this person or idea. It was pretty vague." He squats down and picks up something black. "There you go," he says as he hands me a small, black triangle.

"Oh, look at it! And it was just laying here!"

He winks at me and grins. "Come back sometime and I'll give you a tour on the house, but I see my next group gathering over there, so I gotta go. Annie, good to see you again. You need to have me out to the house for a fish fry before the summer is out. I'll provide the fish."

"Deal! Hey, listen, this means a lot. We're going to find her soon."

"I hope so. The guy didn't seem mean, just a little, oh, I don't know, sad like I said. Besides, he and Eden have the tattoos in common, so that'll give 'em something to talk about."

Annie and I share a look. He's already walking away from us, but I jog toward him. "He had tattoos?"

"Well, to be fair, I only saw the one, but it was a pretty big one. A shark, big, like twelve inches, all black and gray right at the base of his neck. Stuck out above the neck of his shirt. Talk to y'all later!" He hastens his steps toward the group that is headed his way.

I wait while Annie meanders to me and then past me, heading for the parking lot. She asks, "Did he say our guy has a big shark tattooed on the back of his neck?"

"Yeah. But in the video from The Sea Snake, didn't his hair come down over the back of his neck?" We look at each other. "Wait, that wasn't hair. It was a tattoo!" I hurry toward the car. "Surely the police know about the tattoo, right?"

Annie rushes to the car as she digs her keys out of her shorts pocket. "I'd imagine they do, but if not, maybe it'll help." We pull out of the parking lot as the air conditioner blasts us with warm air. By the time it's cooled down, we are back on the main park road and I've heard back from Charlie.

"Yes, they knew about the tattoo, but it doesn't have any gang affiliation and looks to be an old tattoo. So far it's not led them anywhere."

I tell Annie what I'm typing: "Tommy thinks the guy has been here before. Could Ted have done the tattoo?"

"Good thinking!" Annie says.

But then I have to tell her Charlie texted back that they'd already asked him and it wasn't one of his. After I think for a minute, I say, "You were at the news conference. Did you hear someone gasp when the picture of the guy came up in the video?"

She cocks her head and thinks. "You know, I didn't remember that, but just now when you asked, it sounded familiar. Yeah, I remember wondering what was so shocking, but then I didn't think about it anymore. Why?"

"Charlie and I both heard it. We wondered if someone in the room recognized the guy. I'm wondering if someone recognized the tattoo. I'll run that by Charlie."

He texts back, "Could be."

Almost immediately I get another text from Charlie beginning in all caps, "DON'T SAY I'M ASKING, but have either of you talked to Aiden?"

I type, "I haven't. I'll check." To Annie I say, "I'm going to text Aiden. Have you heard from him?"

Annie looks over at me and then turns to wave at the rangers in the entrance building as we leave the park. "No. I was just thinking it's been the longest since this started that I've not heard from him, but then again, he was pretty mad at me about the whole fight with Kerry on TV. Ask Charlie if he's seen him."

I'm already typing, so I send her question and get nothing in return. The back-and-forth stops immediately, and there's not even the three little dots that tell me Charlie's typing something. I lay my head to the side, facing out the window. Big tears well up and run down my face. This is just too much. Eden's been gone a long time with no word. What if she never comes back? How will Ted and Kerry go on? And Aiden? He loves her. I know he didn't hurt her, but there are all kinds of innocent people in jail. I saw him fighting with Holloway. Everybody in the coffee shop saw them fighting. And what if he pushed Holloway down and Eden saw that? What if she attacked Aiden? I shake my head. No, this is all crazy to think. How did everything go so wrong?

I sniffle, and Annie asks, "Are you crying? Did Charlie tell you something else?"

Keeping my face turned away, I just shake my head. He told me not to say anything about Holloway, besides why give Annie more to worry about? She drives on to my house and pulls into the driveway, where we both sit and let the tears roll.

Annie heaves a ragged breath. "I'm just so

tired. And so scared. Where is she? She has to be somewhere. And you're right to be worried about this hurricane. It's turned into a big one, and if it hits, will we ever find her?"

I turn to stare at her. "But you said—"

"I know what I said!" She jerks open her door and yells, "I'm no weatherman! Why in the world would you listen to me?"

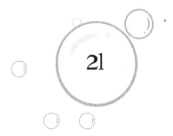

21

Our phones buzz as we're walking up my front steps, but before we can look at them, we hear a whoop from inside. After a quick halt in our climb, we dash up the rest of the stairs and into the house.

"They found her and she's fine!" Ted shouts at us from where he's running up the staircase. Before he can open Eden's bedroom door, it's flung open, and Kerry is standing there in shock.

She's paler than before, and her mouth hangs open. Her wide eyes go from her husband to the rest of us, then down to her phone in her hand. "She's alive?" Then she falls onto her husband, sobbing. He eases her back into the bedroom and shuts the door.

After a moment of silence, the rest of us

begin letting out held breaths and hugging each other. Well, I hug Galena, but I'm not touching Fiona. We are talking over each other as we wait for an update on the television. Tamela, Lucy, and Cherry come rushing into the house, all grins, even with happy tears streaming. Lucy hugs Annie, then me. "We heard the news and came straight here! Apparently one of the news helicopters caught the ambulance racing to them, and so it was out of the bag."

"Ambulance?" Annie asks. "We were told she's fine."

"She is, but it's always a precaution," Cherry says as she turns up the volume on the television. "There she is!"

I pound halfway up the stairs, yelling for Ted and Kerry to come down. "Eden's on the TV!"

They are right on my heels coming down, and we give them seats in the front. The shot is from a helicopter, but it's easy to spot Eden sitting in the open doorway of an ambulance with Aiden standing beside her. They are the only ones not in uniform. She has on a faded orange T-shirt I remember from the back seat of Aiden's car. It hangs longer than her short skirt, and when they zoom in on her, above the stretched-out neck I can see the tight, sequined top she wore out of the house on Saturday. Eden is talking and talking, but the best part is she's smiling, even laughing as she grabs Aiden and hugs him.

Finally I tune in to what the newscaster is saying about Eden being found by her boyfriend, Officer Aiden Bryant.

Annie gasps. "Did you hear that? Oh, that boy!"

Ted jumps up from his seat and wraps his long arms around Annie, then sits back down. Kerry just keeps staring at the screen. "I wonder how he knew where to find her?" she asks, and her voice is hard.

Lucy kneels on the floor beside Kerry and whispers to her. Annie has wandered off to answer her phone, so I don't think she heard Kerry. I'd like to think it was just the response from an overwrought mother, but it had a definite tinge of accusation.

I look around, then step over to Galena. "Where's Cathy?"

"She went for a walk since Kerry was sleeping. I should call her." Galena pulls out her phone and walks into the kitchen. I take another deep breath, then go back to the TV. They're talking to some of the police officers, but no one is saying much except that the kidnapper is not in custody, so they keep their comments to the fact that Miss Church is in great shape both mentally and physically and will be on her way home soon. Once everyone there has had a chance to thank everyone else, they begin walking away from the microphone. Cherry mutes the television, though not before I see the promo for the next story: "Lewis: First Monster Storm of the Season?"

Well, at least there was a question mark.

"I told her there were deviled eggs, so she wants to come here first," Kerry mumbles to me from her seat at my kitchen table.

"Of course. So, is she really hungry?" We haven't heard anything yet about where she's been except that she was found at a storage facility up in the Kingsland area.

Kerry smiles and shakes her head. "No. She just said she's tired of prepackaged food and wants real home-cooked food. She didn't talk long. Just wanted to know where we were." Kerry starts to cry. "Oh, Jewel, I just knew she was… was…"

I rush to hug her. "Hush now. You were scared. Appropriately so." I pull a chair close, and she looks at me.

Her eyes are clear and focused on mine.

"No. I knew she was gone. Knew it. I never imagined her coming home." Her voice fades away, her eyes lose focus, and she looks down. "Oh, I should change out of all this black."

"Eden won't mind," I say, but she cuts me off as she stands abruptly.

"I mind. I can't let her know I gave up hope." She yells, "Ted, I need some other clothes!"

He yells back, "I brought you a bag. It's upstairs." Then he walks into the kitchen, beaming from ear to ear. "Miss Jewel, is it okay with you if we freshen up a bit upstairs? I don't have new clothes to change into, but a quick shower would feel pretty good before she gets here."

"By all means. But they'll be here before too long, so hurry up." I laugh as they rush, and I can't believe how much lighter we all feel.

Ted and Kerry still look tired after their showers, but you can tell they feel better as they wait the final few minutes to see their daughter. Annie and I are standing at the edge of the living room while the rest of the ladies are in the kitchen getting ready to feed everyone. Cathy stopped in for a moment to give Kerry and Ted a hug, but decided to go back to the inn and rest. Galena and Fiona are still here, as are Lucy, Tamela, and Cherry. Outside there's a lot of newspeople and even some townsfolk. A big cheer tells us Eden is here, and I can't stop the tears from flowing. She bursts in the front door, Aiden and Charlie on her heels, and everyone is beaming and crying and hugging.

Eden finally holds her hands up. "I heard there are deviled eggs? And some other real food? The doctor that checked me out said I'd probably crash before long due to the drugs still in my system. Right now I feel like I'm in a dream, so how about we get some food and then I'll tell you what happened and how Aiden is my knight in shining armor and I'm never letting him go!" She grabs the young man and kisses him.

I see her parents frown and look at each other, but I decide that's their problem. "Everyone, there's plenty of food. We'll let Eden and her family and the officers go first through this door, then move out the back door of the kitchen back in here. There's plenty of seating for everyone."

Charlie steps to my side. "I'm going to head out; I still have work to do. I think this guy is halfway to Canada by now, but we're going to catch him."

"Still no idea why he took her?"

Charlie shakes his head. "No. Craziest thing I've ever seen. He treated her like a friend. Like it was a joke, except we can't figure out what the punch line is. But we will." He bends his head close to mine. "Eden doesn't know about Holloway yet. Don't say anything."

"Charles," Fiona purrs, coming up behind him. "Charles, darling. You need to eat something. Keep your energy up. You've worked so hard." Her familiarity with him, the way she's got one hand on his back, the other softly squeezing his shoulder, makes me take a step back.

I start to agree with her and tell him to eat something, but I just take another step back, then another, until I'm in the kitchen.

The Greysons can handle whether or not Charlie eats.

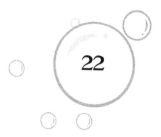

22

"I can't believe that was a fake Facebook account. It really looked like him, just younger." Eden has finished eating by the time we are all seated with our own plates and drinks, so she's ready to tell her story. We'd offered to let her take a nap, but she said she was more than caught up on her sleep thanks to the pills she was given throughout the time she was gone.

"As Jewel probably told y'all, I had already been drinking when I came in to get changed and go back out to meet Jimmy." She squeezes Aiden's thigh. "He wasn't nearly as cute as you. And I'd been drinking, but you, sir, were drunk when you showed up at The Sea Snake causing a scene. I was more than happy to go somewhere quieter with Jimmy—which we all know now was a huge mistake." She draws in a deep breath. "I felt like I knew him because of us talking on Facebook, and he was so nice at the bar. I know, I know. I've always thought I could handle myself. I thought I'd know I was in danger, but I had no idea."

Her eyes tear up, and she reaches out to her mom and dad. "I'll never be that reckless again. I was so stupid. Anyway, I drove us down to the beach. He said he'd Ubered from his hotel because he didn't want to drink and drive. See, doesn't that sound responsible?"

Annie huffs. "When what he really wanted was to get you off somewhere."

"Momma, just let her talk," Aiden reminds her.

But Eden nods. "Yes, Miss Annie, you're right. He wanted me to drive off so there was nothing for y'all to follow. And I did. He had some little bottles of wine in his backpack, and we drank those at the beach. Then I was driving him to his hotel, which he said was up in St. Mary's because it was cheaper. He was on his way to help his grandmother down in Melbourne get ready for the hurricane, and everything just seemed like it fit." She pauses and bites her lip. "Except I remember thinking at times things didn't quite fit, but I think the drugs were already working on me.

I started feeling really drowsy. I guess he put something in my wine. He said he should drive, so I pulled over, and we changed somewhere out on A1A before we turned north on 17." She swallows. "When he got in the car, he was messing with the seat belt, I thought, but he was actually putting a zip tie on my wrist and attaching it to his belt. I was half asleep and drugged, I guess, because I didn't really care. But somehow I must've felt things were off because that's when I started writing on the door of the car with the colored ChapStick I had in my pocket. He was talking about how he wasn't going to hurt me and I'd be home before Wednesday. He promised me I'd be fine."

We are all so quiet. It's hard to remember that she *is* fine and is here. All I can think about is how close this came to turning out horribly and how at the time this was happening no one even knew she was missing.

She tries a laugh. "And I am fine. I woke up in this travel trailer with boards over the insides of the windows in the middle and back section and a partition at the front. Jimmy hung out in the front driver's seat with earphones on, listening to music most the time. And he read a lot. Plus, there was a stack of old paperbacks for me to read when

I wasn't too sleepy. He'd go out occasional-
ly and get food, but mostly we ate from this
huge box of chips and crackers and cookies.
Nothing refrigerated or cooked. There was
a bathroom and shower with a towel and
washcloth for me. The bed had sheets and a
pillow." She shrugs as she looks around at us.
Then she pulls back to look at Aiden. "Tell
them. It was fine, wasn't it?"

He grimaces. "For a prison. That's what it
was, you know."

She sighs. "I know, and I still have no idea
why."

It's strange, but it's almost like she's defending her kidnapper. I've seen something
like this on some television shows, but it's
super creepy in real life.

Ted speaks up. "But couldn't you have
just gotten out and made a run for it? Or at
least yelled out the door?"

"Oh. No, I was, well, I was…"

Aiden answers, "She was chained to the
camper. One of those nylon-covered steel
cables around her waist locked onto a connection bolted to the frame. No way could
she get out without bolt cutters. The chain
allowed her to move around but get nowhere
near the door or any uncovered window. The
camper was really clean. I mean, there was

nothing except what he'd brought for her in it. No utensils or anything to use as a tool."

Ted blanches and leans back. Kerry shudders and drops her head. Then she suddenly looks up at Aiden. "What if you hadn't found her? He'd left. The food would've eventually run out."

"No, Mom, Jimmy swore he'd be calling to let people know where I was by Tuesday night. He told me from the very beginning all I had to do was stay there until Tuesday night. He left this morning and said for me to just sit tight and I'd be home soon." She leans against Aiden. "But I sure am glad I didn't have to wait another night. My super cop found me!"

"Well, Momma helped," he says, and we all look at Annie. "When Momma said she thought the campground would be a good place to hide someone, I kept thinking about that. But of course we didn't find anything in any of the campgrounds. Then at some point I passed one of those big storage places that had this room along the edge for campers and boats. Of course they'd been looked at, but for some reason I just couldn't shake the feeling I needed to look more, so I kept driving around to all the storage facilities I could find. Apparently military bases have a lot of storage places due to the soldiers needing to store stuff when they're deployed. Some of the places I looked around were huge. Then at one place I was going really deep into their back junk area, and I spotted a camper all by itself. I noticed there was one of those orange power cords running through all the junk to it. It was all by itself, back behind some old metal storage units that didn't look like they were in use. Somehow I knew she was there and didn't hesitate to take a crowbar to the door to get it open." He turns pink as he looks around at his admirers, then adds, "But I had to call Charlie for bolt cutters to set her free."

Eden hugs him again. "I didn't mind that so much. It was nice to have a few minutes alone with you. I was sleeping and didn't hear him breaking in until he was shouting my name. Jimmy gave me the last sleeping pill just before he left. He wouldn't give me water unless I'd take the pill, and honestly, sleeping was better than waiting once I realized I couldn't get out." She pushes Aiden's hair back from his forehead. "I felt like Sleeping Beauty being rescued."

Aiden goes from pink to red.

Ted reaches over to shake the young man's hand. "I'm very, very humbled by your persistence, son. You are a credit to not only the police force but our town. Hell, our state. I'm proud to know you."

Kerry sniffles. "You never gave up hope, did you?"

He shakes his head. "No, ma'am. I just felt she was out there waiting for me."

Eden grins. "Well, you and those deviled eggs. Are there any left?" she asks, bounding up from the couch. We all laugh and move around. We're feeling the need to step away from the drama, so we disperse a bit. I pick up a couple of discarded napkins and cups and head to the kitchen.

"What's with her?" Lucy asks me, pointing back into the living room.

Turning, I can see that the only one who hasn't moved is Kerry. She still seated, staring at the spot where Eden had been. "I think she's upset that she thought Eden wasn't coming back."

Lucy nods. "I can see that. But I wonder why she was so sure. It was kind of weird how fast she gave up hope."

"Yeah." I haven't told anyone except Charlie that I think Kerry was self-medicating, which I'm sure wasn't a good idea. I hand her the trash. "If you'll throw these away, I'll see if I can get her interested in some dessert."

"Good idea on dessert." Lucy leans in closer to me. "Then let's get all this food and all these people out of here so you can get back to normal. You've got to be as sick of Fiona Greyson hanging around as I am!"

I furrow my eyebrows at her. "Who?"

Lucy laughs and swats at me. "Girl, you're getting more Southern by the day!"

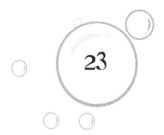

23

"I will never take a full refrigerator for grant-ed again," Eden says, pulling her head out of ours and turning around, plate in hand. "I'm glad they didn't take all the food to the shelter."

"Well, we got rid of a lot of it, but I'm surprised by how much was eaten. I have to admit, it was nice to not have to think about food the whole time. Your parents are wel-come to come eat supper with us, you know?"

She rolls her eyes as she sits beside me at the table. "Not tonight. The paramedics said those drugs will still be in my system a few days, so I'm too tired to handle them. Besides, they need to be at home togeth-er. Honestly, it was worse for them, for all of y'all, than it was for me. It must've been how groggy I was, but I always felt that I was okay."

"Was your mom feeling any better when they left?"

Eden folds a thin piece of ham and takes a bite. "She seemed to be. I don't understand how she got it all so wrong. I mean, I knew she'd be worried, but I imagined her flitting around telling everyone I'd be fine. She's always the optimist. I also imagined my dad driving everyone crazy. Checking back on Facebook, I can see he did that."

"But he got the word out, and that's when the video from The Sea Snake came to light. You looked pretty comfortable with that guy. You said this Jimmy didn't set off any heebie-jeebies at all with you?"

"None. He never touched me inappropriately or raised his voice the whole time. I told the police it was like he was doing a job, yet he seemed sad to be doing it? It was like he was almost apologetic to me. Even in the bar, except for putting something in my drink probably, he was nicer to me than Holloway and Aiden were that night."

This is the first time Holloway's name has come up, and while I want to ask questions, I don't. Maybe he was in on it with Jimmy? Maybe they were accomplices. I have to remember to text that idea to Charlie later. But now to change the subject. "Why do they think he's headed to Canada?" I finish my last bite of potato salad and push my plate away.

"I told them the names of the books he was reading. Most were thriller and adventure novels, but there was one about the wilds of Canada and one about the Alaskan wilderness. Plus, he mentioned disappearing into the woods when he was leaving this morning." She flops back into her seat. "Gosh, that was just this morning? Seems like a lifetime ago."

"It sure does. Oh, hey, it's eight. Time for the hurricane update." I pick up my phone and find the site for the weather guy Annie told me to listen to instead of the folks on national TV. She and the other ladies helped me fill gallon jugs of water, some for drinking and some for flushing the toilet if the power goes out. They gave me a checklist of nonperishable food ideas, and I'm going shopping in the morning to round out the last of the church casseroles. We also placed a next-day online order for batteries and the stuff they'll operate. I have a small fan, flashlights, and lanterns coming on Wednesday. Plenty of time, they tell me.

I feel ready but not ready at all. However, it looked like the hurricane was moving away from the coast on the last update, and so I'm anxious to see the latest news.

"Yep, look. It's moving away, heading up north of us. Whew." My shoulders drop, and I stretch my tight neck muscles.

Eden chuckles. "You'll get used to it. Some seasons you don't hear a thing, and then other years it seems like there's one to pay attention to right after the other. You can't let them get to you."

I click off my phone and lay it down. "Whew," I say again. "I'm really relieved. To have you home and the storm going away… now I'm exhausted! But listen, what do you think about your birthday party? We don't have to do it, but I kind of want to celebrate you even more now."

She bounces in her seat. "Yes. Please. I've even held people off from coming over here or me going out by telling them we're having a party on Saturday. Besides, I think it'll help Mom get back to normal." She stretches and yawns while I take our plates to the sink.

"You go upstairs and I'll take care of our plates and start the dishwasher," I tell her. "You're going to the police station in the morning, right?"

"Yep. Full story again, but on tape. I think they hope my mind will clear on some of the foggy parts with a good night's sleep." She stands and comes to hug me. "Thank you for all you did to find me and to help my mom and dad."

"You're so welcome. But honestly Cathy Forsyth was really who helped your mom the most."

"Mom mentioned her, but she wasn't here today. I'd really like to meet her."

"I think she just crashed after you were found. She really hardly slept at all and was at your mom's beck and call." I close the dishwasher and start it up.

Eden hands me a towel to dry my hands on. "And we both know firsthand what a handful my mother can be. I'm about to drop. Hope I can make it all the way upstairs."

"Me too." I turn out the kitchen light as we move into the living room. "I'd hate to have to carry you." I laugh as I pat Eden's back. "Go on up to bed. I'm going to sit here a minute and text my kids about Lewis moving out to sea."

She trudges up the stairs. "See? Just like a true Floridian, calling it by name. Good night and thanks again."

Her door closes, and the house is quiet as I stand still and drink it in. Hard to believe it was just this morning I took the casserole to Annie's and we had the press conference. There was the trip to St. Mary's and being on the beach talking to the shark guy. But ending the day with Eden home makes it all worth it. Now even the storm is no longer a worry, so it's really peaceful as this exhausting day ends.

Dusk is my favorite time of day; I love the gloaming. Stepping onto the front porch, I walk to the right, where I can look out into the streets of my old, old neighborhood. Lamps in windows begin to glow while the street-lights slowly push away the day. Through the drape of blue gauze descending, the trees and houses lose their edges, their definition, and the windows grow brighter. The blue fades to a soft gray, then a more solid gray, and before I know it, all I can really see are the lights. The windows and the lives inside them. The streetlights and what they fall on.

So much thankfulness wells up in me that I find my throat tight and my breathing shallow. I turn and leave the dark outside.

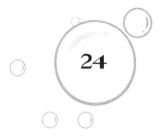

24

"I'm so mad I'm spittin' nails!" Annie says as she carries her travel mug of coffee to the pocket park bench along Centre Street, where we're getting together quickly this morning. Lucy's office is just around the corner, and she was the one with the shortest window of time, so she chose the location. We are a few blocks away from Sophia Coffee, so until the other shops open at ten, this block is pretty quiet, with open parking spots and few people.

Annie settles on the wooden bench beside me while Tamela and Cherry are on the one sitting at an angle to ours. The three of us have water bottles and are sipping them to hold off the early morning heat. We're in full shade from a tree overhead and the building between us and the sun, but it's going to be a scorcher today. As usual for August in Florida.

Tamela rolls her eyes at Annie's anger. "We got the gist of that last night in your texts—oh, there's Lucy."

Lucy's wearing a tight, beige skirt and a sleeveless, navy shirt. Thanks to tennis she doesn't have to worry about the state of her upper arms like the rest of us. Excuse me, like the rest of us except Annie. Annie says we're women of a certain age who live in Florida, where sleeveless shirts are a necessity and our arms are just what they are. I never thought about it much before moving here, but that's before I realized just how white the undersides of my arms are.

Anyway, Lucy squeezes in next to Cherry on their bench. "Okay, I've got fifteen minutes. Annie, can you talk quickly without a lot of sidetracking?"

Tamela rolls her eyes again, and Annie gives her a glare. "I'll try, but y'all feel free to get me back on track. Okay, I was so relieved we got Eden back that I didn't realize just how angry I am that someone thought they could just take a couple days out of her life, out of all our lives, and then hightail it off to the woods up north. Who was this guy? The police need to get on a stick!"

I interject. "Eden went to talk to them this morning. The interview's supposed to be really in-depth and on tape, she said."

Cherry shakes her head at me. "Why haven't they done this already?"

"I think they wanted to let some of the drugs get out of her system. I mean, I know she was happy yesterday, but didn't you think she was a little too happy? Too calm? She said the doctor said it would take a couple of days, but even this morning I noticed she seemed more like herself."

"Silly me," Cherry says. "I mean, I'm the nurse; you'd think I would have thought of that. Plus, yesterday was a very emotional day, so I guess the police know what they're doing. Do you know if they got any more clues off the camper?"

I look for anyone else to have an answer, but they don't. "I don't really know much of anything else. Aiden picked Eden up this morning, and he was in uniform." I peek sideways at Annie. "Is he okay with Charlie?"

She harrumphs. "For now. Charlie needs him while he tries to wrap this all up before that loser's trail goes cold. However, afterward, he's looking at some time without pay.

He says Charlie just keeps glaring at him, so he's in for a rough ride. Deservedly so! One good thing from all this has been having Annabelle around more. I miss that girl, but she's loving her job in Jacksonville. She's covering—"

Lucy snaps her fingers. "No. Another time we'll talk all day long about Annabelle but not now. What I want to know is, why Tuesday? Eden says this Jimmy kept saying she'd just need to stay there until Tuesday. That's today. What's happening today? And, in fact, she didn't stay until Tuesday. She got free Monday. Did that mess something up?" She looks around at us. "Someone needs to look at the calendar of the town or Eden's schedule. Maybe Sophia Coffee or places she goes when she's not working. Jewel, is there anything about today you can think of?"

I shake my head, but then suddenly Cherry leans forward. She purses her lips, barely opening them like she doesn't want to say what's coming next. "Okay, this might really be off base, but could Eden be involved?"

"What?" the rest of us exclaim.

She holds up her hand. "Just think about it. Could she have done it to maybe get Aiden back?"

Annie has drawn in a big breath through

her gaping mouth, but she's not saying anything.

Tamela and Lucy are scowling, but their scowls are loosening as they wonder. I close my eyes, lie back against the bench, and think. "No," I say, bounding upright. "I just don't think so. Sorry, Annie, but she was not, in any way, happy with Aiden after I came home from Erin's. He seemed to not be on board with a breakup, but I'm pretty sure she was ready to move on."

Cherry nods. "Okay, I was just wondering."

There's an awkward pause as we let our thoughts of Eden being part of some conspiracy dissipate. We take sips of our drinks or look at our phones.

I see Lucy check her watch, so I speak up. "I'll check Sophia Coffee and see what's on their schedule for today. I'll even see if there's anything going on there with the other employees—wait, does everyone know about that Holloway guy from Sophia Coffee?"

Annie nods and looks around the group. "I told y'all about him. That he liked Eden and was following her around. Remember? Anyway, the police were looking for him and he's dead!

Tamela squeaks, "He's dead?"

Lucy leans forward. "I heard he was out drinking, fell, and hit his head. Managed to get home during the night, but died in his sleep. What does this have to do with Eden?"

I add the pertinent information. "He fell in the parking lot of The Sea Snake Saturday night."

Annie hisses, "Remember the blood?"

"Oh!" The others exclaim.

Cherry asks, "Did he have anything to do with Eden's kidnapping?" Annie shakes her head but adds a shrug. When they look at me, I do the same.

"We must find out. Add it to our list," Lucy says. "Now, where were we with our assignments?"

I raise a finger. "I was saying I can check with the coffee shop people about today's date and I'll speak to Kerry and Ted. I have to talk to them about the party anyway, which is still on for Saturday night. Kerry is taking care of the food, Ted the drinks, and I'm doing the rest, so we've got it handled, I think. Everyone's invited."

Lucy stands up. "I've got to go. Okay, we know what Jewel's doing, and I'm going to look into the town's schedule. The rest of you?" She plants those toned arms on her hips and waits.

Tamela stammers, "For the party?"

Lucy tips her head at us, her short, blonde hair falling forward in disbelief. "No! About finding out who took Eden and why. I know—Tamela, you can have Hert talk to his police friends. See what they're thinking. They like telling Hert stuff. Have him run the whole Tuesday question by them and ask about the guy who died."

Annie rolls her eyes. "Why am I not surprised Hert has gotten chummy with the police? He'll be mayor of the town before long!" Then she gives us all a sideways leer. "But I thought that was Jewel's venue—you know, sweet-talking Charlie." She winks at me, but my attention is drawn to Lucy, Cherry, and Tamela's quick gasps. Annie notices, too, and demands, "What? What's going on?"

Tamela presses her mouth shut. Cherry leans back, shaking her head. Lucy drops her hands from her hips, looks at her watch, and clears her throat. "Okay, I guess I figured you two would know, but, uh, Fiona is, well, she's been seen at Charlie's new house."

"That two-timer!" Annie explodes. "He's getting a piece of my mind!"

I force a laugh and swat at her. "Annie, she's his wife."

Her face crunches in confusion at me, but

then she smooths it out. "I guess, but, well, I don't know. This just isn't what I thought was gonna happen." She frowns as she catches our eyes. "I just really, really, really don't like that woman."

Tamela echoes, "Really?"

We all ease a bit with a chuckle, and Lucy waves as she walks away. "Text me whatever anyone finds out. See you at lunch tomorrow. Upstairs at The Turtle Shell."

"So, what was going on at Bellington Manor last night?" Cherry asks after Lucy walks away. "I stopped by the hospital because I left my lunch box there on Sunday. While I was at the desk, they had a canceled call from the ambulance crew. They'd been called to Bellington's, but help had been refused, so they were calling in to say there'd be no transport."

"What time?" I ask. "I was out on the porch at dusk, but I didn't see any excitement in that direction."

"Martin and I had an early dinner at Café Mango and stopped by the hospital on the way home, so it was about six thirty."

Tamela pulls out her phone. "I'll call Charlotte and ask if she wants a ride to lunch tomorrow. Then we can see what she has to say." Since she's put the phone on speaker, we can hear it ringing.

"Hello, Tamela," Charlotte says when she picks up. "Decided to be proactive and call me instead of making me wait for you on pins and needles this week?"

"Good morning, Charlotte. Yes, I was wondering if you'd like a ride tomorrow."

"I don't know. Are we still slated to climb that steep staircase at The Turtle Shell and sit upstairs? You know I'm not going if that's still the plan. And then there's my telling you last week I wouldn't be coming because of a prior commitment."

Tamela screws up her face and grits her teeth for a second, but then takes a breath and answers sweetly. "Oh, that's right. You aren't coming this week. You have a doctor's appointment. I can't believe I forgot. That's why Lucy has us upstairs."

The salty old woman says, "I can believe it, considering that's not really why you called. So, are your nosy friends there? You have me on speakerphone, so I assume they're gathered around, wanting to know what I know about last night."

We all stare at the phone like it's a snake. Then we hear her evil chuckle. "Bring me a cheese danish from that coffee place and I'll tell you all I know." She hangs up.

"I'll get the danish since I'm parked on the other side of Sophia Coffee," Annie says. "Anyone else want anything?"

Cherry looks at Tamela. "Do you think she meant all of us? I'd love to see her house."

"What's she gonna do," Annie demands, "not let us in? Turn us away?"

I nod. "Absolutely she would. But I think she wants an audience, so I think it's fine for us all to go." I stand and pull a five-dollar bill out of my pocket. "Can you grab me a couple of the biscotti? They're Eden's favorite, and she'll need a pick-me-up after her morning at the police station."

Cherry puts an arm around my shoulder. "Plus, she'll have to sit and talk while she eats it, right?"

I pat her hand. "Well… there is that."

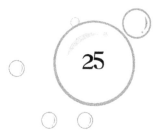

25

"So now I've seen the cottage that Charlotte's always complaining about," Cherry says as we leave the beautiful back garden of Bellington Manor. "It's really charming. Well, with a tinge of creepiness." She whispers, "But I think that's more because of its occupant."

Annie doesn't whisper at all. "You are correct. She's a nightmare, and she lured us here under false pretenses!"

"Not entirely," Tamela says. "We did find out the ambulance wasn't for Frank or Galena but for one of the female guests. But you're right: I think she just wanted to know what we knew about Eden's abduction."

"I wonder if it could've been Cathy," I say. Looking back at the huge house and inn, I think about what Charlotte told us. Frank called the ambulance, but when they arrived, the woman he'd called it for refused treatment. Charlotte said the EMTs had parked by the inn's back entrance, so she could hear the discussion from her front door. Frank told them the woman was unconscious but then woke up and had closed herself in her room. Charlotte told us she'd later snuck in, and in the big, leather guestbook, she saw that there are currently three female guests. One is Cathy, and she wouldn't name the other two. She'll never give you everything. Secrets are just one of her many ways of retaining control.

Tamela's phone ringing makes me look away from the inn.

"It's Hert," she says. She talks to him, then hangs up. "Hert isn't letting any grass grow under his feet. He's having lunch down at Manteo's with a couple of his police buddies who are off duty. I'm going to walk by, spot them, and join them for a few minutes. I can ask our questions and then leave to let Hert get all the details."

Cherry has been texting while Tamela talks. "Well, I've got my afternoon booked. Jo's off after they do lunch, and we're going hunting for sharks' teeth with that Tommy Tompkins at three thirty." She looks up at us.

"Jo's been wanting to get more into the whole beach thing, so this is as good a starting point as any. Plus, I didn't know how else to help."

Jo is Cherry's daughter who's recently left school and moved in with her folks. I ask, "How's her new job going? She did get hired at The Isle, right?"

"Thanks to Lucy talking to Davis. Helps to know one of the owners. She's starting out on the lowest rung possible in a kitchen, but at least it'll help her know if she wants to go to culinary school. It's a great opportunity to work at such a nice resort."

Annie lifts her hand as if to testify. "All my kids got their first jobs because of who I know around here. Then it's up to them to either shine or flame out. Jo will be just fine! We should go there for lunch sometime to support her. We can't afford dinner."

I laugh. "Yeah, I wanted to take the boys to the resort for their birthdays this summer. I'm so glad I checked the prices first. But lunch did look doable."

Cherry steps up to her car. "I have to go change and pick up Jo. I'm excited about my day with her; learning anything to do with Eden will just be the cherry on top."

"Tell Tommy I sent you," Annie says.

"He's a little skittish around folks he don't know. But he'll warm up."

Cherry waves at us as she climbs in her car. Tamela says she's going shopping along Centre before it's time for her to meander by Manteo's, a mostly outdoor restaurant with picnic tables and a pirate ship for kids to play on, not to mention fabulous, fresh seafood. She heads off as Annie texts Aiden to ask how Eden's doing.

We chat on the sidewalk while we wait for his answer. When her phone chimes, we stop talking for Annie to read it out loud. "She's still talking. Doing good. Can you bring us lunch?"

We look at each other and smile. Can we drop into the police station doing a good deed and nose around a bit? "Of course we can!" we say at the same time.

Did I imagine Charlie did a double-take when he saw me with Annie? He seems a little awkward. Or does he? Now that I've spent more time around Fiona, I can't imagine him wanting to be with her. But then, he is and he has been, so…

Aiden takes the sack of deli food we picked up for him and Eden from his mother while I set out a platter of cookies from Karen's Bakery. "These are for everyone," I say, but there's really no need as the gathering from all corners has already begun. It's like when you open a bag of chips on the beach and seagulls appear out of nowhere.

Annie hustles over to Charlie's office door, which is half open. Behind her she's motioning for me to follow. I drag my feet but arrive there in time to hear him say to her that he's really busy and doesn't know much more than he did earlier. However, that doesn't stop Annie from plopping down in one of the chairs across from him. When I screw up my courage and join her in the chair closest to the door, he sighs, walks around the desk to close the door, and then goes back to sit in his chair.

He stares at Annie and asks, "What can I help you ladies with?" I don't think he's actually looked at me yet.

"You know nothing more about this creep that took her?" Annie demands. "What in the world are you people doing?"

He bristles. "He was good. Not just some random good ol' boy playing a prank." He closes his eyes. As he opens them, he leans forward, his elbows on his desk. "We're thinking he's military of some kind because of the way he left no trail. That is hard to do."

Annie and I share an amazed look. Then she whispers, "The military took her?"

He smiles. "No, not the military. Just that it looks like he's been in the service. Things Eden told us also. His efficiency and manners. Plus, it feels like he was on a mission, something he was familiar with doing." He definitely doesn't look at me when he asks, "You heard about that guy Holloway?"

Annie nods vigorously. "I didn't care for the man, but it's awful that he died. Do you think it had anything to do with Eden's abduction?"

"Eden says it doesn't. She said he followed her and Jimmy outside but that he just watched them go." He sits very still, which I've discovered is one of Charlie's tells. I know he's not telling the whole truth.

So I press. "But you don't believe that's all that happened, do you?" He glances in my direction, then shrugs. I continue. "This Holloway was into some bad stuff, so what if he hired Jimmy to abduct Eden?"

Now he's looking at me. He quietly asks, "To what end?"

"For money. To, you know, sell her. I've seen the movies."

Annie gasps and lies back in her seat. "Lord save us. I can't even think of that. Jewel!" Then she realizes Charlie isn't saying anything, and she starts to fan herself. "No, I just can't…"

Charlie starts to stand. "Ladies, I need to get back to—"

I scoot forward on my chair. "Okay. Forget all that. You mentioned it not being a prank. Wasn't 'prank' one of the words Eden wrote on her car door? You know, in the ChapStick?"

"She says no. She can't remember what she was writing, but she says it never entered her head that it was a prank. She's still pretty fuzzy on details. After she eats, we're going to take her out to look at the car to see if she can figure it out. The pictures of it haven't helped her." His forehead creases as he thinks for a moment. "There's something emotional here. For all the clues that make it seem like a straightforward mission, there are things that make it feel personal. Have either of you talked to Kerry and Ted today?"

Annie quickly says, "No," then turns toward me. "Jewel is headed over there after we finish here, though, right?"

I nod, and he gives me his attention. "We're planning Eden's party for Saturday night. It's still on." Then my voice peters out. "If you want to come." I look down at my hands, clutched on my crossed knees, and realize I'm as tight as the strings on Lucy's tennis racket. So often I've felt Charlie and I connect, almost read each other's thoughts. It's one of those instant friendships that are so rare, yet we've always walked on eggshells. Now, when it seems like we're close to turning the corner and being at ease with each other, it's like the whole thing is slipping away, little bit by little bit. Or was it ever truly within reach?

I tell myself to loosen up and not be so dramatic, but then Annie says, "If you come, will you be bringing Fiona?"

He leaps up from his chair like she set it on fire. "I need to get back to the questioning." He pulls open his door and motions for us to leave. I hurry out, but Annie takes her time. I'm practically to the outer door before she leaves his office. She stops to have a word with him, and I'm so glad I didn't wait for her. He follows her across the room and, at the last minute, steps away from her toward me.

"Jewel, I need to talk to Kerry and Ted some more, but not in a really official way. Don't want to make them tense. Can you text me when you get there, and then would it be okay if I show up just in a concerned kind of way? There's something I can't put my finger on. You remember what all I told you about Ted's causing trouble?" His voice is low and personal. He's standing too close, and I just want to get out of there, so I nod and push out into the cool, softly lit entryway. Annie follows me straight to the front doors and then into the blazing sunshine of a Florida afternoon.

We hurry to the shaded sidewalk, where Annie grabs my arm. "So, what'd ya think about that?"

"So he might bring his wife to a party. Why would I think anything about that?"

Annie scrunches up one side of her mouth. "Not that. I mean, I don't know what to think about that. But those pages laying on Charlie's desk. You know, the ones with all the shark tattoos."

It's not the afternoon sun that makes my face heat up. Here I was supposed to be seeing what I could find out about Eden's kidnapper, and I was worried about, well, other stuff. "No. I didn't see those."

She's looking at her phone. "See? There they are, and that one is circled."

"You took pictures? Of police evidence?"

"He was busy watching you storm away, so I knew he wouldn't notice what I was doing. I'm getting pretty good at this kind of thing, don't ya think?" She's beaming at me and holding out a very clear picture of three shark tattoos, one of which has a circle drawn around it.

"Yes. You are getting pretty good. Send me that and I'll show it to Ted."

Whether I'll text Charlie remains to be determined.

I might've lost his number.

Now that's silly. As soon as I decide I'm not interested in him, I go and act like a lovesick teenager. Of course, I have his number. And of course, I'll text him.

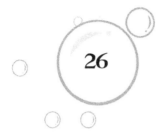

26

Annie drops me off at my house since I have the biscotti for Eden to put away; plus, I could do with a bite to eat. Annie tried to talk me into going out to lunch, but I'm just not in the mood. I think the last few days are wearing on me. I'm going to forage for leftovers in my very full refrigerator and then sit in the quiet and cool house, focusing on the good things: Eden is safe and the hurricane is out to sea.

A scoop of chicken salad and some veggies from a platter someone brought make the perfect lunch. With a full stomach, I try to close my eyes and relax, but my prickly skin just won't let me. You know, that prickly skin thing that says you shouldn't relax. The one that keeps you from settling down when you know you really want to. The thing that keeps you getting up to check on the kids when they're small or makes you turn on the weather channel when you know, *know*, the hurricane is way far away by now.

And yet—there it is.

What is it still doing out there in the Atlantic? Shouldn't it be halfway to Canada by now—though I guess I've never heard of Canada having hurricanes. And why are we in that one cone? The other predictions suggest it's going up north to maybe the Carolinas or Virginia but not here. I'm surprised by how worked up the forecasters on TV still are. They've got to be drinking a lot of coffee or energy drinks to keep up this level of anxiety. Speaking of which, I can feel my heart beating faster, so I mute it and then force myself to turn the television off.

No one seemed upset in town today; Annie didn't even mention getting gas, though I guess she's still got a full tank. Everyone keeps saying they'll tell me when to worry. At least the storm's away from Craig in South Florida. I'll give him a call tonight and bring him up to speed on everything here. I let him and the kids know about Eden, but I haven't really talked to him this week. I push up from my chair, collect my plate and glass, and move briskly into the kitchen. With my mind in gear and my body in motion, the prickly sensation is gone. Funny how that works, although it's not so funny when I know I really could use some rest. I think I'm just too geared up from everything. I say out loud, "Everything is fine," a few times, though I'm not sure how much I believe it.

I know I'm tired when I consider driving instead of walking to see the Churches. Signs, their tattoo parlor, is only two blocks over and a block up from me on Centre Street. It's so hot out there, but parking is a bear, so I might as well take my time and walk. I set out, staying on the shady streets as much as possible. This path takes me to the corner where the Bellingham Manor Inn is, and as I cross the street, I spot Galena sweeping her front porch.

"Hi," I say with a wave, and then I purposely turn up the sidewalk. "Seems warm to be out sweeping."

She stops and waits for me to climb the steps. "Seems even warmer to be out taking a stroll."

I laugh. "We're both right."

"Sit down if you've got a minute," she says, motioning toward the wrought iron tables and chairs along the front of the house, in the deep shade of the big porch.

"Nice furniture. Good and heavy."

"Yes, but such a pain to move when we have a storm."

I draw in a breath. "Okay, I have to ask. No more concern over the hurricane? I mean, I looked just now and it's still out there."

"You just have to ignore it until you're told otherwise. Sometimes they hang out there forever, it feels like. Or they suddenly move where they said it couldn't."

"Like to here?" I feel my eyebrows close in on my hair line.

"No." She laughs. "No, I mean, it could, of course, but seriously, you just have to trust your friends and realize these storms do not move fast. If things get hairy, you'll have plenty of time to get out. We're not down south where you can't get inland easily. One hour north and you're deep into South Georgia. Just relax."

"Everyone keeps saying that." I lean back into the thick cushions. "I bet you have to talk down your guests all the time. Cathy was as bad as I was."

She nods but doesn't say anything for a while. Then she looks at me with concern on her face. "Maybe that's some of it. I hadn't thought of her being upset about the hurricane. This thing with Eden really drained her. I think being with Kerry so much was hard."

"Oh no! She seemed to be glad to be helping her. Kerry can be a handful. I hope we didn't foist her off on Cathy. I was so worried about Eden, but I probably should—"

She cuts me off. "No, you shouldn't feel bad at all. Cathy wanted to help. It's just that it brought back so many memories of when she lost her son."

"She lost a son? Oh, Galena, I had no idea."

Galena peeks at the front door. "I wanted to make sure that was shut," she explains, then turns to me. "She doesn't talk about it much at all, so there's no reason for you to have known. That's one reason I was hanging around your house. I was afraid it would be too much for her, but she was adamant about wanting to help Kerry. Cathy felt very alone when her boy passed, she always tells us." She leans in my direction, whispering, "But her husband is very private and kept everyone away. Frank and I went up to the funeral, and everything was just beautiful but very formal. Cold, actually."

"What a shame. Cathy doesn't seem cold at all. The opposite actually."

"I've noticed that this trip. She seems more settled. She says she feels closer to him near the ocean because he loved it so much. I think that's why she'd like to live here."

"Has she found any houses she's interested in?"

"Well, she didn't get to look this weekend, and now she's kind of lost interest. And, well…" She looks around at the door again. "She was kind of sick the other night."

The ambulance call. "Oh really? What was wrong?"

"I'm not exactly sure, but it was very scary. Honestly, Jewel, I think she took something. She went up to take a nap once Eden had been found, but then I couldn't get her on her phone or when I knocked on her door. We of course have keys to all the rooms, but we have never had to use one when a guest wouldn't answer." Galena realizes she'd raised her voice and lowers it again. "But we had to. I was scared to death!" She reaches out and lays a hand on my arm. "Frank even called 911."

"That is scary. What happened?"

She lifts her shoulders and shakes her head at me. "She finally woke up and then was so upset that we'd called the ambulance. She refused to see them. I brought her up a tray of food, and then she locked us out again. She said she just needed rest."

"How is she today?"

"Fine, I suppose. She came down and ate a bite of breakfast, but she wasn't very talkative."

"Do you think she'd see me? Is she staying much longer?"

"She's supposed to be leaving today, but she hasn't said if that's still her plan. I think she'd like to see you. Want me to check?"

I think about Charlie waiting for me to text from Kerry and Ted's. Then I smile at her. "Sure. Tell her I stopped by and would love to say goodbye since she's leaving."

Galena returns my smile, pats my hand, and gets up. "I'll be right back."

I use the time I'm waiting to check the weather maps, and I see that Lewis hasn't moved in the last hour. I might not be made for living in hurricane country.

"Jewel?" Cathy says, and I step up to the door.

Cathy is standing in the doorway with the screen door closed between us. "Thanks for stopping by, but I'm not feeling well." I can see she's holding the door shut. "I'd hate to spread whatever it is to you. You've been very kind. Kerry is so lucky to have you."

"You're the one that was so much to help to her. I'm on my way to see her. I know she'd like to thank you herself. Maybe you can stop by there later if you get to feeling better."

"No. I have to go. Bye," she says as she turns away. From the darkness inside, Galena shrugs and then motions that she's going to follow Cathy back up the stairs. I wave at her and turn to walk down the front steps.

Cathy didn't look good. Nowhere near as perky as she's looked every other time I've seen her. Maybe she really is sick, but... I'd swear when I mentioned her going to see Kerry, she shuddered.

I even shudder as I step out into the sunshine. Cathy looked like a ghost behind the old screen door. It's shaken me, so much so that I stop on the other side of the inn's brick fencing to take a minute and catch my breath. When my phone vibrates, I pull it out of my pocket.

Tamela says the cops Hert had lunch with had nothing to add that we don't already know. As for today being anything special, she says they couldn't think of anything. She stopped in at Sophia Coffee, but they had no ideas either. She said they miss Eden, though, and are all looking forward to the party on Saturday. In another text, Lucy gave the same report about the city calendar.

I guess we're down to me talking to Eden's parents. Oh yeah, and I guess we shouldn't count the police out. I smile as I text Eden to see if she's headed home yet. Sounds like she gave them a lot to work with, so maybe there will be a breakthrough soon.

As I near Signs, I debate going around to the back and up the stairs to the apartment or going through the shop. I stop to read Eden's reply that she's getting a glass of wine with a friend on the beach. She may take a walk after, but she'll let me know when she's heading home.

I draw in a deep breath. Her going to the beach sends a little shock of fear through me. Didn't she just meet up with a friend and end up kidnapped? But no. She'll be fine. I know she'll be fine.

As I push open the front door, the smell of the antiseptic reminds me of a doctor's office. Ted is alone behind his desk in the back, and he grins to greet me. "Hey there! Come on in. I'm just catching up on some paperwork."

I walk back through the stations and lean on the high counter. "How are you? Thought

I'd stop to talk over some party stuff with Kerry. Is she upstairs?"

He looks over his reading glasses at me. "Yep, and you can't imagine how happy I am to see you. She needs to get on to planning the party and off the past couple of days."

"She doing any better?"

He shrugs. "I don't know. Maybe. Why she can't just be grateful and move on is beyond me. Eden's perfectly fine. She apparently never was in any danger. Maybe I'm just being Suzy Sunshine, but I'm so grateful that I can't worry about all that other stuff."

"But I get Kerry wanting to know why, you know?"

"I do. I do. But we might never know why. Then what?" He puts down his pen and stretches. "Don't get me wrong, I'm not pushing her or anything. I'll give her all the time and space she needs. But she's gone from beating herself up about that whole situation with Victor Morrison to beating herself up for thinking Eden wasn't coming back."

"Do you think the whole ordeal with Victor is why she was so quick to assume the worst about Eden?"

"Yep, I do. How about you?" When I don't answer right away, he looks back at me. "What are you thinking, Miss Jewel?"

"I'm not sure. Not sure of much these days. Can I go up?"

He nods at me, but then I remember the picture. "Oh yeah, I wanted to show you a picture."

I pull up the shark tattoos and point to the one that's circled. "I think Eden must've picked this one out as the one on the back of the guy's neck."

He takes my phone. "Oh yeah. Black mako. Pretty popular tattoo subject." He points to his left. "I have a couple like this up on my board. But like I told Charlie before, I've never done a shark on anybody's neck, front or back."

I step over to the board. On a framed poster are all kinds of drawings of sea creatures, including the dolphin Annie is considering getting on her ankle. "So nothing unusual about a shark tattoo?"

"No. Especially not on an island, much less a tourist destination. Some people are fascinated by sharks. Dolphins are the most popular, though, especially with women." He grins. "I think that's what's making Annie hesitate; she doesn't want to do what everyone else does. Also, the sea turtle seems to get more popular every year, especially around here."

"Okay." I turn toward the stairs. "When Charlie shows you the picture, can you act like it's first time you've seen it?"

He winks at me. "Oh, Miss Jewel, now you're asking me to lie to the police? You are getting rambunctious. Next you'll be wanting a barbed wire tattoo on your bicep."

I shoot my finger at him. "You'll be the first to know."

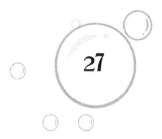

27

"Are you sure Galena said Cathy had lost a son?" Kerry is seated across from me at her kitchen table. We've written out all our plans for the party, so now I've broached the past weekend by telling her about my conversation on the porch of Bellington Manor.

"I'm positive. She didn't mention it in all that time you spent with her?"

Kerry concentrates on the doodles she's drawing on the paper in front of her. "I really don't think so. Surely I would've remembered that." She looks at me. "Don't you think?" Then she looks past me as the door from downstairs opens.

Ted steps in, followed by Charlie, who is not in uniform.

Kerry goes still. "Charlie, what's wrong? Is Eden okay?"

Both men jump to explain that everything is fine. Charlie smiles at her. "I just wanted to stop by and see how y'all are doing. Everything good here?"

My smile at Charlie is a closed-mouth one, and then I scoot my chair back. "You can have my seat. I should probably be leaving."

But Kerry reaches out and grabs my wrist. "No, you don't have to leave. Right, Charlie? It's just a friendly visit, right? You said Eden is fine."

He assures her again that everything is fine, and then Ted motions toward the living room. "Let's sit over here. I could use a break. Can I get anyone anything?"

We say no, and then all four of us are settled on the couch and two chairs in the middle of the apartment. Ted is in the chair beside me, and he leans forward, his elbows on his knees. "Have you found out anything more about what happened?"

"Not a lot. This Jimmy seems to have training for this kind of thing. One of the ex-military guys told me it looked like something a professional would do if they just wanted to take someone temporarily out of a situation. Can any of you think of any reason for that to happen to Eden?"

Kerry's furrowed brow is matched by her husband's, and they shake their heads at each other. She looks at Charlie. "So this wasn't some random thing. This guy wasn't just out having fun or playing a prank?"

"No. Doesn't look like it. And we figured out the word Eden wrote on her car door wasn't 'prank,' but 'shark.' She can't remember why she wrote it. We think it must've been because of the man's tattoo."

Kerry hugs herself as if she's cold, though this apartment is anything but. "What is it with these shark tattoos? First that whole threat of a lawsuit, and now this man with one. They must be cursed." She lifts her chin. "Ted, take them out of our shop. We will no longer do shark tattoos!"

She's grown louder while the rest of us got quieter. From the looks on Ted and Charlie's faces, I realize they hadn't made that connection before now either. Then Ted says, "That kid with the heart condition? But that went nowhere."

Charlie asks, "Do you have the paperwork on that handy?"

Kerry points to a file cabinet with a painted wooden tray on top of it. "I filed it away with the other stuff from the first investigation when the young man died. We call it our dead files." She gasps as she catches herself. "Not dead because he died, but the stuff we don't think we'll need again. I believe in keeping records." She gets up and bends down to pull open the drawer and go through it. She has on a long, gauze skirt with a tropical pattern, and it swirls around her as she turns to Ted. "Here it is. Should be the last thing in the file."

"His name was Bruner. Tiburon Bruner." Charlie reads while the rest of us watch him.

Kerry sinks back into her place on the couch, but moves closer to Charlie as she looks toward the papers. "I just don't see how this could have any connection," she says.

Charlie stops reading and closes the file. "Um, is it okay if I take this to look at more closely?"

Ted and Kerry nod as he stands up, and we can all tell the energy in the room has shifted. Charlie looks like he can't get out of here fast enough. He's headed for the downstairs door by the time the rest of us stand. He lifts the folder in our direction as he pulls open the door, but he doesn't say a word before he's gone.

I dart to the table to pick up my notebook with the notes for the party, shove it into my bag, and start for the door as well. "I have everything I need for the party. We'll talk soon. I better be going." Then I'm out the door and running down the stairs after Charlie.

He saw *something* in that file, and I want to know what it is.

All I see, though, is his car pulling out down the block. See, this is why I should've driven. The station is too far to walk to. I don't have any choice but to go home and get my car. As I start walking, I check my phone, which I'd silenced while I was talking to Kerry. The only notification is a text from Lucy saying she can't find anything significant about the date. As I'm looking down reading that, I bump straight into Cathy Forsyth.

"Oh, Cathy! I'm sorry. I should be watching where I'm going, but I'm kind of in a hurry."

Her laugh is weak. "Well, I'm glad I bumped into you, literally. I must apologize for my brush-off this morning. I've so enjoyed getting to meet you."

"Me too. I hope you're feeling better." We move to a shaded part of the sidewalk, but she doesn't look like she's hot or cold. She looks numb and a little out of it. Maybe Galena's right and she is taking something.

"I'll be fine. Now you have a good afternoon. I'm going to drop in on Kerry and tell her goodbye as you suggested. Then I'll be on my way."

She's wearing a white, flowing sundress, which really washes out her coloring. Her only makeup is a shiny, pale-pink lipstick, which is a first. Every time I've seen her, no matter how tired, she's always had on full makeup and worn more structured clothes. Maybe she really is getting into beach life. She gives me a soft, quick hug, and then she moves on down the sidewalk. I watch her for a moment, but she doesn't look unstable on her feet. I'm glad she and Kerry will be able to say goodbye.

But I need to get to Charlie and find out what's in that file.

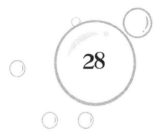

28

Annie is backing out of my driveway as I cross the street. I wave and yell to get her to stop. "Hey! Hey!" She can't hear me with her windows up and air on full blast, so I jog in her direction and smack the back of her car as she pulls away from me.

She throws on the brakes, and I almost run right into the car.

I jog around to the passenger window, and she rolls it down. "You almost gave me a heart attack! I thought I'd run over some jogger. Lord, girl, what are you doing? Get in here before you pass out. Your face is all red."

"Thanks. We need to go to the police station," I manage to say as I scramble into the seat.

Annie grins and throws the car in gear as she bombards me with questions.

I hold up my hand. "Let me catch my breath and enjoy the air for a minute."

She stops the questions but keeps talking—and driving. "Why does that dropping in on people never work for me? I'd like to be more spontaneous, but no one's ever home when I try it."

I turn to give her my "you've got to be kidding" look. "Annie. The last, very last, thing any of us need is you being more spontaneous. But I am glad you decided to stop by. I can't believe how hot it is out there—and that humidity!" I look down. "My shirt is soaked, and I wasn't running or even jogging. Just walking fast."

Annie eyes me more closely. "You sure you want to go into the police station looking like that?"

I pull down the visor and see in the mirror that my hair is just as wet at my shirt and my face is covered with red splotches. "I guess."

She tsks. "But you know, Charlie might be there."

"Charlie better be there. He ran out of Kerry and Ted's so fast he had to have seen something in that file folder." I take a deep breath and lean close to the vent. "Remember that young man that died after getting a shark tattoo? His family wanted Ted's shop investigated, but it was determined the tattoo had nothing to do with his death?"

She slaps the steering wheel. "That's right! It was a shark tattoo. Did it match the one that man who kidnapped Eden had?"

"Well, no. And Ted didn't even do that one. But it's a connection, right?"

"A connection? Possibly. But more like a coincidence I'd say." She pulls into the parking lot at the police station.

I fluff my hair, trying to dry it. I'm pulling my shirt in and out for the same reason. "Well, it's got to be more than a coincidence because when Charlie saw something in the folder Kerry gave him, he jumped up and left. I couldn't catch him and was heading home to get my car."

"Well, let's go see what it is," she says as we climb back out onto the hot asphalt. We not only step into heat, but into a quiet so deep that it is only interrupted by the hum of air conditioners. We walk up the front steps of the station and into the entrance hall with me leading the way. We wave at the receptionist, whom we've seen several times over the last few days, and I point to Charlie's office. She nods, and we head back. I stick my head in his door, and he's standing behind his desk. We walk in, and he smiles.

"Hot out there?"

I drop into one of the chairs. "Yes, and you probably knew I was following you."

He sits down. "I guess I would have if I'd thought about it." He looks up at Annie, who is still standing and surveying his desk. "Anything you want to take pictures of? Anything you missed when you were here this morning?"

"Me?" Her blue eyes widen in their innocence. "Not at all." She sits down, and he just shakes his head.

Then he looks at me. "You're not going to believe this. That young man that died last year—"

Annie interrupts. "Last year? I'm pretty sure Jewel told me it was a couple years ago."

Charlie frowns. "It was last year." He looks from her to me. "Matter of fact, exactly one year ago. He died one year ago today."

"Lucy was right!" Annie says. "She thought it had something to do with today being important."

"But we couldn't find anything," I say as Charlie nods. He says they couldn't either.

"We're doing searches on anything to do with this Bruner guy, and we should have more to go on soon." He stands. "Thanks, but I've got to get back to work. I'll keep you in the loop."

Annie frowns when I hop up, though, with a smile, I motion for her to get up too. She says, "We can't just stay inside the loop from here?"

Charlie and I say, "No," at the same time. Someone calls for him, so he moves out into the larger room. I nudge her leg with my knee. "Get up. We at least need to go out into the entryway. Cherry's trying to get a hold of me, and I don't want to call her back in here."

That gets her to hurry, and I dial Cherry back as we rush out into the quiet entryway. "You called me? Aren't you on your shark tooth hunting thing?"

"Yes, but I can't get service on the beach, so I walked up onto the boardwalk to the parking lot. My text to you still wouldn't go through. We're way up at the north end of the island inside the state park. Anyway, I'd talked to Mr. Tompkins, the shark tooth guy, about the kidnapper while we waited for the others to get here. Then once we were on the tour, he kept watching these two little brothers, and like a lightbulb going on, he said the man had mentioned a brother, but he'd completely forgotten to tell anyone."

"Great. I'll tell Charlie. Bye."

Annie shouts, "Wait!," then pouts at me when I hang up anyway. "You didn't tell her about the connection with the boy that died."

"Because she doesn't know about any of that. I told you about him and the tattoo by mistake, remember? The others don't know, and I don't feel like explaining it to them now. Let's go tell Charlie about the brother. Then we need to go somewhere quiet. I feel like I need to think all this through."

When I pull open the door, we're greeted by noise and action. Charlie sees us and waves us over to him. "This Tiburon Bruner has a brother who was with the Special Forces and got out earlier this year. Exactly the profile we've been looking for. We've put an APB out on him." He holds up a clear photo of the guy we've been calling Jimmy in uniform. "I'll get Eden in here to positively identify him, but I'm confident this is him. Name is Finn Bruner."

Officer Weber, who'd been at my house looking for the creepy notes left at Kerry and Ted's shop, looks up at the picture. She tucks a hank of her dark hair behind her ear. "That's weird. His name is Finn and his brother is Tiburon?"

We all look at her. Charlie nods. "Why's that weird?"

"Finn, you know, like shark fin, and Tiburon is Spanish for 'shark.'"

Annie tsks and shakes her head. "Doesn't that beat all. Some names you never hear, and then they all of a sudden become popular."

Now we shift to look at her. "Tiburon?" I ask.

She rolls her eyes and folds her arms. "No, silly. Finn. First that boy on that music show *Glee*. Then there's that woman Cathy, you know, Galena's friend, from Atlanta? Her son. And then my sister's first grandson born last year was named Finn. Not my cup of tea, but it's right cute, I guess."

Charlie pounces. "Woman from Atlanta?"

I think back. "That *was* her son's name, wasn't it? Finn and, uh, something kind of funny. Sounded like a little boy's name."

Annie nods. "Yeah, and I'd never heard it, so it didn't stick with me like Finn." Her eyes pop open. "You think this could be the same Finn?"

I grab Charlie's arm. "Galena told me this

afternoon Cathy lost a son. It's got to be the boy with the shark tattoo. It's got to be. "

My hand drops as Charlie moves around the desk and starts barking orders to find Cathy Forsyth at Bellington Manor Inn. But then my eyes widen and I shake my head.

"Oh no. She's not there. She's with Kerry and Ted."

Charlie's face turns to stone.

I cover my mouth with my hand as I realize this was more about Kerry and Ted than about Eden. Now it looks like they are the direct targets. Annie and I move to the side to be out of the way of all the commotion. Then I see Naomi, Ted's friend whom I met just yesterday, waving at me. We skirt around the edges of the room as the officers rush out.

Naomi is seated behind her desk in a side office with a big window looking out into a courtyard. She hugs me as I rush in. Then, as I begin to introduce her to Annie, they hug like Southerners do when they've known each other forever. Of course they know each other. What was I thinking?

Annie pats her back. "Don't you worry none, sweetie. Ted'll be just fine. This Cathy is not much bigger than a gnat."

Sinking into her desk chair, Naomi sighs. "Yeah, but it sounds like she's crazy. Nothing good ever comes from messing with an angry, crazy person." She lifts her eyes to us. "Especially an angry, crazy woman." She turns to the side of her desk. "I've got a radio here, so we'll know in a minute if things are okay over there. Y'all might as well have a seat."

I close my eyes, cover my face with my hands, and lean forward, elbows on my knees. I moan. "This is all Cathy's doing?" I drop my hands and sit up straight. "The notes! I forgot about the notes. I bet she's the one who told Kerry to burn them."

Annie rocks back and forth in her chair, hugging herself. "Lucy and I looked in that wastebasket. All that was left were ashes. Then you and I went down to the beach to talk to Tommy Tompkins, and when we got back, Eden had been found. I hadn't thought about those notes again until right now." She then begins to explain what the notes are to Naomi, but Naomi waves a hand and says, "Jewel and I already talked about those notes earlier. She came to my house looking for Ted."

Annie cocks an eyebrow at me. "You went to Naomi's looking for Ted?" When Naomi looks away, Annie mummers, "You'll have to tell me what you know about them? Everybody wonders."

With a frown to try and make her be quiet, I turn away from her.

Naomi taps the radio. "Come on now. Tell us what's going on."

But when it comes to life, it's just Charlie's voice saying that the Churches are fine. Mrs. Forsyth stopped in the shop, acting like she didn't feel well. She talked about being glad she was there when they thought they'd lost Eden, and they thanked her. She then told them goodbye and said she was going to say goodbye to the ocean. Charlie ended by saying that he's sending officers out to the beaches and that he's heading to Bellington Manor.

"Praise the Lord," Annie says with a laugh. "Ted and Kerry are all right."

Naomi nods at her, but then shakes her head and frowns. "Something don't sound right. I'm not sure what it is, but I'm not going to look a gift horse in the mouth. This woman needs to be found, stat."

We agree with Naomi, then tell her goodbye. As Annie and I are driving away from the station, my phone rings. "Hi, Cherry. Are you done with the shark tooth hunt?"

"Yeah, but we're still on the boardwalk where the pier used to be, and Cathy Forsyth is here too. She's really upset."

"Oh! Stay there. Let me call Charlie." I hang up and dial him "Cherry just called from the beach at the state park, and she says Cathy Forsyth is there too. They're on the boardwalk where the pier used to be. She says Cathy is upset."

Like I said earlier, having friends means you don't have to ask because you already know the answer. It also means you don't have to give them instructions because they're already doing what you want.

Annie is flying down A1A, headed to the park.

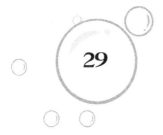

29

Heavy, moss-laden limbs fly by above us as we well exceed the park speed limit of 15, then 25 miles per hour. We take the turn leading out of the forest toward the beach campground, then turn into the large, open parking lot beside the boardwalks to the beach.

We get out and jog along the hot boards in the full sun. When we get to the bathhouse, there's no one up top, but Cherry and her daughter, Jo, wave at us from the ramp leading down to the beach. We turn toward them as Cherry points to the overlook behind us. "She was there. Crying and shouting when we came off the beach. I tried to talk to her, but she was inconsolable. She kept talking about a son, I think. Tibby?"

"That's it," I say. "Tibby. Yes, it's a long story. Where is she now?"

Jo runs down onto the stand and waves her hand for us to follow. "When the rangers got here just before you, she suddenly made a run for it. The rangers are down there with her on the beach. Come on!" We follow her through the small dunes and see Cathy sitting on the beach with two park rangers squatted in front of her, talking to her. A beach patrol buggy pulls up on the sand, and we hear running feet behind us on the boardwalk. Officers descend on the area and begin pushing people back.

Cherry says as we hurry along, "So, like I said, she was talking about her son, and well, I think she planned to jump off the pier." Charlie and Aiden hear that as they join us on the path.

"That matches up with the note she left at the Bellingtons'. You ladies stay back," Charlie says over his shoulder as they pass us on the way to Cathy.

We slow down to give them some space, but after Charlie talks to her, he motions us over. I think he's saying just my name, but it would take more than the few police here to keep Annie and Cherry away. He meets us outside the circle of officers and talks low.

"Paramedics will be here soon, but she said she wanted to talk to you."

I walk up to her and then sit on the sand. I pat her back and lean over to look at her. "Hey there."

"Oh, hello, Jewel." She lifts a hand toward the water. "No one told me the pier was gone. It was here when I visited last time. But it's gone. I had such a good plan."

"We don't want you to hurt yourself."

"No, the plan was to *stop* hurting. Tibby was all I had. Finn is, well, he's a good son, but he's more like his father." She looks at me and smiles. "My first husband was Julian Bruner. He was a marine biologist and kind of famous."

I smile back. "Let me guess. He specialized in sharks."

She's sifting sand through her fingers, and she watches it fall for a minute. "Yes. Finn idolized him and is so much like his father, so passionate but hard to connect with. I was always closer to Tibby, and Finn adored his little brother. When we lost Tibby, well, Finn just closed himself off. He was already in the military and living overseas, so I've been completely alone. I mean, I had my husband, but, well, he never grew close to either boy, or to me for that matter. He just wanted…"

She shrugs and digs her hand into the sand again. "Tibby was right. I should've never left Julian."

When she turns back to me, her eyes are full of tears, and she looks like she'll never be happy again. "I just wanted Kerry to know what it was like. Of course I wouldn't hurt Eden for all the world, but her parents needed to know what it's like to lose a child. Why did they have to give him that tattoo? Tibby was so good at following instructions. He'd been sick before, and he always did just what the doctors said. If Kerry and Ted had said no, he wouldn't have died."

That Sunday at my house comes rushing back to me. The day she stopped by before I knew Eden had been taken. That Sunday, she said, "Please save me." I thought she was talking about saving her from the cocktail hour at Bellington Manor, but was she?

She looks out to the ocean. "It was such a good plan. No one told me the pier was gone."

"Mrs. Forsyth?" Two paramedics come around on my side and face us. One bends toward Cathy. "Let us help you up and get you checked out, okay?"

After a long sigh, she slowly nods. As they help her stand, she says again, "It wasn't supposed to go like this. It was such a good plan."

I scoot out of their way as I hear one paramedic say sweetly, "Then we'll help you find a new good plan."

They lead her over to sit in the lifeguard truck, and Annie and Cherry join me on the sand.

Charlie comes to squat in front of us. "Her note apologized for all the trouble but didn't mention Eden or her parents by name. Probably didn't want to implicate her son in the kidnapping. It was clear she meant to end her life in the ocean. She just couldn't accept her youngest son's death. Needed someone to blame." He clears his throat. "We contacted her husband, and he didn't have much to say beyond the fact that she'd cleaned out her bank account. He also called back to say she'd apparently sold all her jewelry. We're assuming that she gave all the money to Finn for him to kidnap Eden, then disappear. Our military sources said he's the type we probably won't ever find. Especially with that much money."

Cherry gives me a side hug. "So she blamed Ted for her son's death? But the tattoo wasn't responsible?"

"No," Charlie says. "Tiburon had a lifelong heart condition. He didn't report it on the release forms, and he was an adult. The doctors say that there's no evidence of a link, but his mother couldn't accept that. She wanted someone else to hurt like she had. I'd imagine her older son felt he was just doing her wishes. He'd washed out of the military earlier this year for depression he couldn't get a handle on. Not only did his little brother die last fall, but his father, Julian Bruner, died a couple years ago."

I shake my head. "Eden said he seemed so sad. I can't help thinking of him wandering on the beach and talking about the sharks' teeth. It was an awful thing to do, him kidnapping Eden, but I guess he thought it was the only way to bring his mother some peace, maybe himself too. They'd been suffering with it this whole year. Seems like they took the time to put together a pretty elaborate plan. The notes, her purse down in Jacksonville, but her car up in St. Marys."

Cherry leans her head onto my shoulder. "It's all so sad. I'll never forget her running up there and realizing the pier was gone. We were washing our feet at the spigot and getting a drink, and she ran right past us. Then she stopped and started screaming." My friend shudders. "I'm glad she couldn't jump off, but it was so awful to hear her. She was completely shattered."

I shiver and nod. "She kept saying how it was such a good plan."

Charlie pushes up onto his knees. "And it was. By the time we figured it out, well, it would've been too late if the pier was still here. I'm going to go wrap all this up. Send folks home. Mrs. Berry, can you come by, your daughter, too, and give us a statement before you go home? Shouldn't take long."

She says, "Sure." On either side of me, I can sense Annie and Cherry looking up at him, but I don't. He pauses a moment longer, but I stare straight out at the waves until he moves on. I don't have room in my mind for anything else right now.

Taking my friends' hands, I squeeze them as I take some deep breaths. "Annie, can you take me home? This day has been long enough. I need to lie down."

"Sure, hon. Well, on one condition…"

We look over at her, and she cocks one eyebrow high. "Tell me why in tarnation I ever sat down here and then help me get up!"

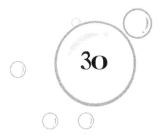

30

"So next week is the week before Labor Day, and we're not doing lunch," Lucy announces. We're upstairs at The Turtle Shell where the tables are all four-person high-tops, so our Wednesday lunch group is spread out at three different tables. "We also won't meet the week after Labor Day, so that's two weeks without our lunches. Feel free to get together on your own, but don't expect an email from me." She sits back down in her metal chair and puts her napkin back on her lap.

Annie screws up her face. "Two weeks? We don't usually take off two weeks in a row. I bet she's going somewhere with Davis. Some exotic island or something."

I shake my head. "Nope. Mackinaw Island on the Upper Peninsula of Michigan.

Oh, wait, I guess that is an island. There's a big, grand hotel there that is very fancy. Davis has a convention for hotel people up there." I lower my voice. "It's very expensive. You have to dress up for dinner."

Tamela is the third person at our table, and she wrinkles her nose. "I bet it's already cold way up there."

"It's called 'refreshing,'" I instruct them. "The nights have a chill, and the days are sparkling bright. We spent a Labor Day weekend in Saugatuck, Michigan, a couple of years ago. It's a little town on Lake Michigan. There are all kinds of fruit orchards, so many apple groves. Everyone is making fruit pies, and the wineries are such fun."

Annie's face is screwed up again. "'We'? Who's we? You and the kids and Craig?"

"No, just Craig and me." I pause, because I'm trying to process this just as much as my friend is. "We have had some fun times. He's always worked really hard, lots of long hours and traveling, so we tried to enjoy our weekends." My throat tightens. "And we did. It was just, without the kids, we didn't really know how to act. What to do. That weekend was fun. I do remember that, but..."

Tamela sympathetically tilts her head toward me. "But what?"

"We fought about what we were going to do when the kids graduated. We never could figure out what was going to come next. How did you and Hert have such a smooth transition?"

Her eyes pop open, and she leans back. "Me and Hert? Well, we just… you know, I'm not sure. We just, uh, kept doing what we were doing but stopped working?" She shrugs. "That's not much help, is it?"

Annie perks up, then says under her breath, "There she is."

"Kerry," I say as I turn and wave her over. "I'm so glad you could come." She's who I was holding the other seat at our table for.

Her hair is back in a braided bun, and she has on a white, button-up blouse and brown slacks. The poor thing looks so nervous. I jump off my chair and meet her with a hug. "Come sit down. I've got a chair for you right here."

Annie and Tamela greet her, and as Kerry sits, she looks around the upper deck area. "Is everyone here part of your group?"

"No." I point to the table next to us and then the one in the corner where Lucy is. "Just those two and ours. You probably know everyone already. Different people come each week."

She holds up a hand at me. "Oh, I don't know that I'll come every week. You know I have to help Ted, and well, I'm just not much of a joiner."

Tamela smiles at her. "We are very flexible. Come if you can, and if you can't, you just don't answer Lucy's email. It's all very casual."

A waiter pops up. "Ma'am, can I get you a drink? I'll be taking food orders in a minute."

Kerry nods and tells him a water is fine. She turns back to our table and clears her throat. "After this awful summer, first with Victor and all that mess, then with, well, you know, I think it would be good for me to make some friends." She swallows like she could really use that water. "Jewel suggested I come to lunch. Thank you," she says with a nod at me.

"I'm glad you could come. It's sure helped me feel at home here. I mean, this has been your home for a long time. You don't need that, but I just…" I cut off my rambling.

"But it's obvious I need friends because apparently I'm not that great of a judge of character." She makes a silly face and shrugs.

Annie reaches across the table and covers Kerry's hand with hers. "You were under a lot of stress, and Cathy Forsyth took advantage of you. You did nothing different than any of us would've done. I'm just so glad Eden is fine."

Kerry licks her lips. "Annie, I asked Jewel if we could sit with you because I owe you an apology. I've already apologized to Aiden, but I was too hard on him. I'd like to blame Cathy, but that was all me. I, uh…" She pulls her hand away from Annie's. "I don't know what to say. He's a good man and a good friend to Eden."

Annie cocks her head, and I watch her blue eyes as she studies Kerry. I know she's trying to decide if Kerry is being sincere. Annie did not like the idea of me inviting Kerry to the group. She might've used the terms "oil and water" and "over my dead body." Finally she gives her a smile and a nod. She picks up her menu and fans it open. "Anyone want to share an order of the seared tuna nachos?"

"I got to thinking today about that trip we took to Saugatuck. Thought I'd give you a call."

Craig chuckles. "That was a fun weekend. We ate so much fruit pie!"

I chuckle too. Outside the night is falling fast. From my high-back chair in the alcove off of the living room, I watch the moonlight weave through the tree limbs. "Can you see the moon from your room?"

"How did you know? I mean, I'm not in my room, but I'm out in the little courtyard area looking at it. Decided I had to come outside and see it."

"Aren't the bugs bad there?"

"So bad I'd miss a moon like this? No, not too bad. So things have finally settled down there?"

I get up and walk barefoot to the back door. "Yes. Thank goodness. Eden is fine. Quieter and more thoughtful. This summer has been pretty frenetic for her and Aiden. They're at that stage where they need to grow up, but they're not sure how to do it. Funny how some kids do that more easily. More smoothly." I step out onto the small back porch. "Oh," I breathe. "It's so warm."

"You're outside too?"

"Now I am. The warmth here is something else, isn't it?"

"It is. I was ready to hate it, but, well, I'm kind of loving it," he says. "Have we become Florida people?"

"I think I actually might be. I really am enjoying it here." I know I let my statement hang in the humid air, but I don't know what else to say. I don't know how to talk to him anymore. Have I ever?

There's a long pause, and finally he says, "I know you are. Listen, I'd like to come up there over Labor Day. I mean, if that's okay with you?"

"Of course it's okay. I mean, none of the kids will be here."

"I know."

Again the conversation pauses. I hear a slap. "Well, there's the bugs."

"Yeah, I'm headed back inside too. It's good talking to you."

"You too. I, uh…" He searches for words, and I wait, not jumping in to supply him with the words or to save him from stumbling as I usually do. I wait. He clears his throat. "I miss you, Jewel. Thanks for reminding me of Saugatuck."

I can't help but grin. "Maybe you can call me next time when you think of a good memory. We have a lot of them."

The relief is palatable in his voice. "Yeah. Yeah, that's a great idea. Well, you have a good night, okay?"

"I will. You too." I hang up and lean against the closed door. He misses me. He actually said he misses me.

This has been a very good day.

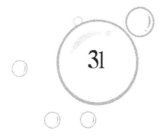

31

The Mantelle Mansion is rocking. This is what this house was meant for. People, lights, music—parties. Walking through the downstairs is difficult with so many guests gathered for Eden's birthday party. The kitchen once again is full of food, but this isn't sympathy food; it's fun food. Kerry outdid herself with baking things both savory and sweet. Her assortment of mini-quiches seems to be never-ending, and she made these peppery spinach balls, which apparently multiply as we eat them. Of course there's a bounty of local shrimp in a huge, glass shell we borrowed from Davis's restaurant at The Isle Resort. Sophia Island shrimp are large and pink, and once you eat them, you are spoiled for any other shrimp. (I never imagined you could tell the difference, but you can.) Ted set up a bar in front of the big, recessed window where he says he thinks there used to be a window seat. I can't believe I never realized that. First thing Monday, I'm getting a carpenter in to see about rebuilding one there. It could become a perfect nook.

The room off to the side has been cleared for the dance floor. The chairs have been pushed into the larger room for extra seats, and Eden says the fact that there are no overhead lights makes the side room great for dancing. It lets people more easily lose their inhibitions and makes slow dancing more private. She has so enjoyed preparing for the party, much more than she would have before she was taken, which isn't surprising after I think about it. Before she was so unsure about life, so ambivalent about everything. And angry.

And while we were worried sick about her, she said she never felt unsafe with Jimmy, or Finn as we now know him. I think that was partially, if not all, due to the drugs he kept giving her. He's still not been caught. Cathy is back in Georgia with a team of doctors in the best mental care facility money can buy. Galena says her husband is mortified and would divorce her if he wasn't afraid of the backlash both on his business and in his social circles. Galena is going to ask permission for me to write Cathy soon.

I make my way toward the dance floor with my refilled glass of wine. Eden is having a blast with some of her girlfriends dancing to a song with motions it seems like most of the people know, so I wasn't joking about the house rocking. I was concerned when Ted and Kerry wanted to pick all the music, but Eden is a big fan of classic rock. Her parents say that's because they raised her right. I can't argue; the music is wonderful.

"Great party," I hear in my ear. I turn, but I already know Charlie is standing beside me. He cocks his head at me and smiles.

I have to agree. "Yes, it is. Lots to celebrate."

"Too hot for walking lately? I haven't seen you out in the neighborhood."

"A party like this doesn't just happen. I've been busy."

"Of course. I've just missed you out and about."

We stare at each other for a moment. "Is Fiona coming?" I ask, turning back toward the dance floor so that I feel rather than see him shrug.

"Fiona is complicated."

A little laugh jumps out of me. "Oh, she is that for sure. And I have a feeling anyone in her vicinity is easily caught up in all those complications."

"True, true."

From my other side my arm is jerked, and Annie whispers, "Jewel. Come here." I follow her tugging, relieved to have a reason to leave Charlie's side, and find Tamela, Lucy, and Cherry standing in a little group.

Cherry lays a long arm across my shoulders. "Great party, Jewel. This place is laid out perfectly for a party. The big main areas, the little nooks and crannies for private conversations."

I turn to Annie. "What's up?"

She won't make eye contact with me, but her grin looks like it belongs to the cat who ate the canary. I thought for a moment she'd pulled me away from the conversation with Charlie on purpose, but now I see she's got something else on her mind. She quietly squeals, "There's a big surprise tonight, and I didn't want you to miss it. There he is," she says.

We all turn to see Aiden walking toward us down the back hall. He winks at his mom as he strides past us straight onto the dance floor. The raucous song is ending, and a low, soft song is beginning, but it seems like the volume has been turned down, and I spy one of Aiden's friends at the speakers Ted set up. The dancers are waiting for the next song, and they part for Aiden to make his way to Eden, who has her back to him. Then I can see in the faces of her girlfriends that they are keeping her turned that way on purpose— until Aiden can get in place.

Then get down on one knee.

She sees him as her friends turn her around, and her hands fly to her cheeks. She has on a beautiful, filmy print dress with spaghetti straps. Its jeweled colors of ruby and emerald accent her hair and eyes, and she looks like a fairy as it floats around her.

Aiden looks up at her, one hand cradling the other, which holds a ring. "Eden Church, you are my dream come true, and I have known it for so long I almost forgot it. I promise I won't forget it again. I will wake every morning grateful for you being in my life and spend every day treating you like the woman that makes my world go round. Eden, will you marry me?"

She reaches down to take both his hands in hers. "Oh, Aiden. I forgot too. I forgot we were made for each other. I don't know how I let it get away, but I also promise to never let it happen again." She grins wide and opens her hands to hold out her left one to him. "Yes. Yes, I will marry you."

He slips the ring on her finger and practically leaps off the floor into her arms. As they hug, the music comes up, and it's an old Carpenters song, "We've Only Just Begun," that takes my breath away.

That was played at my wedding. My wedding to Craig. He'll be here in a couple of weeks, and as I think about that, I feel like I did when we first met. That flush, that thrill. I listen and remember and hold those feelings close. What did Aiden say? They'd been together for so long he forgot it was a dream come true? Craig really was my dream come true when that song was played at our wedding. Him, then the kids, it was all a dream come true, but...

Then the music rises to full volume, and the moment, the dream, I'm standing in right now fills my thoughts. Plenty of time for memories later.

Behind me Annie is being congratulated, and I turn to join the celebration. She's beaming and dabbing delicately at some happy tears. "He asked Ted for permission just this afternoon. I mean, we all know Ted can't keep a secret, so we couldn't give him too long to hold on to it. My boy and Eden have had some very long walks on the beach since she's been home. Some very long, very emotional walks."

I hug her. "I knew they'd been talking a lot, and I hoped it was leading in this direction. Congratulations! I need to find Ted and Kerry."

I see them near the dance floor, but there's a crowd around them and the newly engaged couple, so I settle back into my friends' huddle of joy and laughter.

"Everyone! Everyone, listen!" Aiden is shouting as we turn toward him and the music softens again. "Let's have all the couples up for a special slow song." Everyone claps and cheers as the crowds shift. Martin and Hert aren't far away, and they come to claim their brides. Lucy heads off when she sees Davis is already near the dance floor. Annie and I grab hands, but then her other hand is grasped by her sometime boyfriend, Ray Barnette, and I let go so they can join the fun.

Charlie is walking toward me, and I have to catch my breath. Is he really going to do this? He's going to ask me to dance in front of all these people? I just don't know if… Then the front door opens, and in come Galena and Frank Bellington, with Fiona Greyson in their wake. I watch as the light in Charlie's eyes dies. He looks from me to her, and I can just hear the old Facebook line: "It's complicated." Then, with a big laugh, Fiona pulls a good-looking man wearing a dark suit jacket into the room. As he catches up to her, she presses into him and walks between me and Charlie, never looking at either of us.

The space around us has cleared, but the moment's passed. At least it has for me. I turn and hurry to the kitchen.

Complicated I don't need.

~ ~ ~ ~ ~

"Want to see them?"

"Of course. I thought that was what we were all gathered here for," Annie says to the newly engaged couple. Annie, Kerry, and I are upstairs in Kerry's apartment, enjoying a variety of the leftover food from last night's party.

Eden and Aiden have just come upstairs from the studio, and we can hear Ted hurrying up the stairs to join us. "Wait for me!" he cries.

As Ted rushes into the room, the couple holds out an arm each, and we can all see that the same tattoo graces the insides of the two wrists: a small shark. Eden's voice is thick. "We wanted to remember the boy, you know?"

She's not the only one who is choked up as we think of all we've been through this past week and then of the boy, Tiburon, who got the original tattoo.

We smile at each other, and then Kerry reaches over and takes Annie's hand. "Remembering is good. Forgiving is better."

Book 5 in the
Southern Beach Mysteries Series
is coming soon!

THE
GATOR
DID
IT

Don't miss the first 3 books in the series!

Check out all of Kay's Southern Fiction
and Mysteries at
www.KayDewShostak.com
and she loves being friends
on Facebook and Instagram with readers.

Here is the first chapter of book one in the
Chancey series. Book ten in the series releases
in 2022.

CHAPTER 1

So how did I get stuck driving with my
daughter, the princess, during one of her
moods? Rap music, to pacify her, adds to my
sense of disbelief. Carolina Jessup, you have
lost your mind thinking this move can work.

Rolling hills of dry, green grass and
swooping curves of blacktop lead us to a
four-way stop. Across the road, sitting cad-
dy-corner, is the sign I found so adorable last

October. When we still owned a home in the Atlanta suburbs and moving hadn't entered the picture.

"Welcome to Chancey, Georgia. Holler if you need anything!"

A scream of "Help!" jumps to my lips, but that might disturb her highness. Maybe she's asleep and won't see her new hometown's welcome.

"Holler? Who says 'holler'? Who puts it on their sign for everyone to see?"

Nope, she saw it.

With a grimace, my voice rises above Snoop Dog, or whoever is filling my car with cringe-inducing music, as we cross the highway. "Honey, it's different from home, but we'll get used to it, right? And Daddy's really happy. Don't you think he's happy?" She dismisses my question, and me, by closing her eyes and laying her head back.

I stick my tongue out at the sign as we pass. I hate small towns.

Savannah sighs and plants her feet on the dashboard, "All my friends back home want me to stay with them on weekends." Drumming manicured fingernails on the door handle of my minivan she adds, "Nobody can believe you did this to me."

Guilt causes my throat to tighten. "Honestly, Savannah, I'm having trouble believing it, too." Apparently, she's tired of my apologizing because she leans forward and turns up the radio. Rap music now pounds down Chancey's main street, but no one turns an evil eye on our small caravan. Two o'clock on a Sunday afternoon, there's no one to notice our arrival. July heat has driven everyone off the front porches, into air conditioned living rooms. Bikes and skateboards lie discarded in several yards, owners abandoning them for less strenuous activity, like fudgesicles and Uno.

Jackson is driving the rental truck ahead of my van in which our twenty years of life together are packed tighter than the traffic at home. Oh, yeah, Atlanta isn't home anymore. As the truck takes a curve, I have a view inside the cab. With their grins and high fives, they might as well be sitting on the driving seat of a Conestoga wagon headed into the Wild West. Next to Jackson in the truck is our thirteen-year-old, Bryan. Beside the passenger window is our older son, Will. Bryan is ecstatic about this move. Will just wants to get it done so he can get back to his apartment at the University of Georgia.

We slow to take a turn where two little boys in faded jeans lean against the stop sign post. After Jackson passes, the taller one steps toward the road and waves. I press the brake pedal harder and roll down the window. Humidity and the buzz of bugs from the weeds in the roadside ditch roll in.

"Hey guys."

"You moving here?" He punctuates his question with a toss of his head toward the moving truck lumbering on down the road ahead of us.

"Sure are. I'm Carolina and this is Savannah."

The smaller boy twists the front of his red-clay-stained t-shirt in his hands and steps closer. "Ask 'em."

"I am," the speaker for the pair growls as he shoves his hand out to maintain his distance from the younger boy. "You moving up to the house by the bridge?"

"The train bridge?"

He nods and both boys' eyes grow larger. They lean toward me.

"Yes, you can come visit when we get settled."

Both boys shake their heads and the designated speaker drawls, "No, ma'am. Can't." He pulls a ball cap out of his back pocket and tips his head down to put it on.

The little one keeps shaking his head and finally asks, "Ain't you afraid?"

Savannah moans beside me, "Mom…"

"No, we like trains. Well, we'd better be going."

"You ain't afraid of the ghost?"

My foot jumps off the accelerator and finds the brake pedal. My finger leaves off rolling up my window. "What?"

But they don't hear me. The boys are running toward the house sitting in the yard full of weeds.

Savannah grins for the first time today. "Did he say 'ghost'? Cool." She turns the music back up, lays her head against the headrest and we pull away from the corner.

Ghost? Like there's not enough to worry about.

Tiny yards of sunbaked grass and red dirt pass on the left. Across from them a string of small concrete buildings house a laundromat, a fabric store, and Jeans-R-Us. Chancey's version of an open-air shopping mall. Hopefully, Savannah's eyes are closed as I speed up to catch the truck. Over a small hill, the truck comes into view along with a railroad crossing. A smile pushes through my worries as I think of the grin surely on my husband's face right now.

For years, Jackson talked about moving and opening a bed & breakfast for railroad enthusiasts, railfans, in some little town. Now, a lot of people fantasize about living in a small town. I believe those are the people who have never lived in one—like my husband.

Only five weeks ago, he came home with a job offer from the railroad. We'd already experienced life with the railroad in our early married life. When we finally tired of his constant traveling, he took a job with an engineering consultant and we moved to the upscale suburbs northwest of Atlanta. Railroad job, or no, nothing was getting me out of the suburbs.

Then I find condoms in Savannah's purse, freak out, and accidentally make his dream come true. Well, the small town part of his dream, but the B&B is not happening. Things won't get out of hand again, not with me focusing.

At the railroad underpass there is no stop sign or light, but Jackson and the boys are stopped anyway. Arms poke out of both windows of the truck cab. There's no train coming but Bryan and Will spent more father-son outings in rail yards than parks so they could be pointing at one of a hundred things of interest.

At first Jackson's train obsession was cute, but I realize now, I'm an enabler. Like the husband walking down his basement stairs when it dawns on him his den could double as a scrap-booking store. Or the wife suddenly realizing her last ten vacations involved a NASCAR event.

Past the railroad yard and up the hill overlooking town, the harsh sunlight is muted by thick, leafy boughs drooped over the street. Shade allows for thick lawns encased behind wrought-iron fences or old-stone borders. Sidewalks cut through the lawns and lead to deep front porches and tall houses. The houses stand as a testament to Chancey's once high hopes—hopes centered on the railroad and the river. As we come to the top of the summit the River runs on our right. Savannah leans forward to look out her window, pushing her dark hair back. Ahh, even she can't ignore the view.

"Mom, you realize we are officially in the middle of nowhere, right? Look, nothing but trees and water as far as you can see. Not even a boat in all that water. I guess everybody's inside watching *The Antiques Roadshow*."

So much for enjoying the view. We turn

away from the river and start back down the hill, taking a sharp turn to our right. A narrow road maneuvers through a green channel of head-high weeds. The road and weeds end in wide-open sky and a three-track crossing.

"Great, a stupid train already," Savannah growls. We can't see the train but up ahead her father and brothers are out of the truck and pointing down the line. We both know what that means.

I put the van into park and lay my head on the steering wheel. My sense of disbelief wars with the memory of the joy on my husband's face. Is it possible for us to be happy here? A train whistle blows as dark blue engines rock past and my head jerks up. Through the blur of rushing train cars I see the other side of the tracks—and our new home.

Frustration cuts through my sadness because someone is sitting on the front porch. Are you kidding me? A drop-in visitor already?

Find the rest of *Next Stop, Chancey* and the other Chancey books on Amazon.com or at your local bookstore.

9 781735 099149